Princess Frederi
Christmas Wish

1. A special first holiday season for my baby son, Leo.

2. Mistletoe hung with care throughout the palace.

3. A beautiful stocking for Leo, embroidered with his name—and maybe one for my new bodyguard, Treat?

4. The ability to stop gazing at Treat from afar!

5. An evening snuggling under a blanket with my sexy guard to watch old Christmas movies.

6. A feast fit for a princess and my prince(s)— Leo and Treat!

7. A father for Leo...and the husband of my dreams?

* * *

ROYAL BABIES:
A new generation of little princes—and princesses!

Dear Reader,

Welcome to Christmas in Chantaine! I'm so happy to be back in the wonderful Mediterranean island country with the royal Devereaux family. Princess Fredericka suddenly finds herself a single mom to a baby with special needs, and she is determined to give him the best life and first Christmas ever. Her brother, Prince Stefan, wants her to stay at the palace, but she wants to make a home for her son and herself.

Her bossy brother relents as long as she'll accept his choice for a bodyguard—former football player Treat Walker. Fredericka finds Treat imposing and intrusive and immediately regrets the agreement she made with Stefan. As the Yuletide season progresses, however, she is surprised by Treat's tenderness with her baby. With each passing day, she feels herself falling for him, but Treat is determined to maintain a professional distance. After all, how could a relationship with a princess ever turn out well?

Join me for this holiday romance that will make you remember there's hope for us all during this loving season of the year.

Merry Christmas,

Leanne Banks

A Royal
Christmas Proposal

—

Leanne Banks

HARLEQUIN® SPECIAL EDITION®

If you purchased this book without a cover you should be aware
that this book is stolen property. It was reported as "unsold and
destroyed" to the publisher, and neither the author nor the
publisher has received any payment for this "stripped book."

Recycling programs
for this product may
not exist in your area.

ISBN-13: 978-0-373-65855-8

A Royal Christmas Proposal

Copyright © 2014 by Leanne Banks

All rights reserved. Except for use in any review, the reproduction
or utilization of this work in whole or in part in any form by any
electronic, mechanical or other means, now known or hereinafter
invented, including xerography, photocopying and recording, or in
any information storage or retrieval system, is forbidden without
the written permission of the publisher, Harlequin Enterprises Limited,
225 Duncan Mill Road, Don Mills, Ontario M3B 3K9, Canada.

This is a work of fiction. Names, characters, places and incidents are
either the product of the author's imagination or are used fictitiously, and
any resemblance to actual persons, living or dead, business establishments,
events or locales is entirely coincidental.

This edition published by arrangement with Harlequin Books S.A.

For questions and comments about the quality of this book, please contact us
at CustomerService@Harlequin.com.

® and TM are trademarks of Harlequin Enterprises Limited or its corporate
affiliates. Trademarks indicated with ® are registered in the United States Patent
and Trademark Office, the Canadian Intellectual Property Office and in other
countries.

Printed in U.S.A.

LEANNE BANKS

is a *New York Times* and *USA TODAY* bestselling author who is surprised every time she realizes how many books she has written. Leanne loves chocolate, the beach and new adventures. To name a few, Leanne has ridden an elephant, stood on an ostrich egg (no, it didn't break), gone parasailing and done indoor skydiving. Leanne loves writing romance because she believes in the power and magic of love. She lives in Virginia with her family and a four-and-a-half-pound Pomeranian named Bijou. Visit her website, www.leannebanks.com.

This book is dedicated to all the parents
who have gone the extra mile, two miles
or one hundred miles for your child's well-being.
Thank you for your love and devotion.
You've made the world a better place.

Chapter One

Princess Fredericka hoped her brother wasn't going to be impossible.

She knew she had made more than her share of mistakes. She'd been a wild child when she'd been a teenager and terrified her family with her antics. Everyone had breathed a sigh of relief when she'd gotten married, because she'd appeared to calm down. In many ways she had, but she'd learned things didn't always turn out the way one expected. She'd managed to make the best of what life had dealt her. Ericka knew her brother Stefan, the ruling prince of Chantaine, however, would have a hard time seeing her as a competent single mother to her adorable son, Leo.

She resisted the urge to fidget as she waited to be invited into her brother's office. She nodded at staff members as they hung holiday greenery and put candles in the window. Ericka suspected the Christmas decorations had been ordered by Eve, her brother's wife. Ericka barely remembered seeing Christmas decorations when she had been growing up in the palace. With the exception of the huge Christmas tree in one of the formal rooms, one might not have known the holiday existed. Of course, the deep chill between her mother and father hadn't helped matters.

Her father, Prince Edward, had been a philanderer and an absentee father and husband. Her mother had felt trapped and bitter. Ericka remembered wishing only that she could run away. She'd done exactly that in more than one way, which was why she suspected this was going to be a messy discussion. Stefan was extremely protective.

The door to Stefan's office finally opened. "Your Highness, Princess Fredericka, please come in," Stefan's assistant said.

She nodded. "Thank you very much," she said, then entered her brother's office while the assistant left the room. "Stefan," she greeted, walking toward her brother. She noticed a wisp of a couple gray streaks on the sides of his dark hair. The burden of his position was obviously weighing on him.

She kissed his cheek and he kissed hers. "How are you?" she asked.

"I'm well," he said. "I'm more concerned about you and Leonardo."

Ericka smiled. "Leo and I are great. I'm happy to be back in Chantaine after spending the last year with Tina in Texas."

"You could have spent the last year here in Chantaine," he said, and rounded his desk to sit in his chair.

Ericka sat in the chair across from her brother, watching him as he tented his fingers and studied her. "I think it was good to be with Tina in Texas during my pregnancy and delivery. She and her husband were supportive, and it was fun having their daughter, Katarina, around. She's quite the spitfire. Little ones put everything in perspective."

"True," Stefan said, giving a serious nod. "I think it would be best for you and Leo to live at the palace."

Ericka's stomach twisted and she bit the inside of her lip. She hated to go up against Stefan but knew it was necessary. "I think not," she said. "I've found a lovely gated cottage and a nanny. I think this will be best for Leo and me."

Stefan frowned. "But what about security? You and Leo need to be protected. That would be much easier within the palace walls."

Ericka shook her head. "The palace isn't the place for me. If you think about it, it's not the place for most of us. None of your siblings live here. I apologize for how this may sound, but the palace feels claustrophobic. I don't want that for Leo."

"He's a baby," Stefan said. "How will he know?"

"Babies sense more than you think. He would sense my tension. Leo and I need our own place. As I said, I have found a wonderful nanny and I've arranged for therapy for his hearing disability."

Stefan pressed his lips together. "Is there any chance you're wrong about his hearing? He's so young."

"No," she said, remembering the grief she'd suffered when she'd learned her perfect Leo couldn't hear. The doctors had tested Leo before she'd left the hospital with him, and many more tests had followed. "He has a hearing disability and I'm determined to make sure he gets the best treatment available."

"I can't believe you don't think living in the palace would make your life easier," Stefan said. "And your son's life safer."

Ericka shook her head. "Don't try to guilt me into doing things your way, Stefan. I have to follow my best inner guidance. I have to be my own expert. I'm counting on you to be supportive."

Stefan sighed. "This situation is going to put a lot of pressure on you. I hesitate to bring up the past, but—"

"You're talking about the time I spent in rehab in my teens," she said. Ericka couldn't blame any of her family for being concerned, but if she'd successfully survived her most recent humiliation, she could handle anything. "I'm lucky I learned to avoid chemicals early on. I haven't had a drink in nearly a decade. I learned to wake up every morning and make the decision that I'm not going to drink or use drugs that day."

Stefan nodded. "It's obvious you've come a long way, but I still don't want you to be overwhelmed."

"I'm going to be overwhelmed at times," she assured him. "I have a baby. Being a mother is new. But I'm a Devereaux and I'm not the weak link you may have once thought I was."

"I never said you were the weak link," he said with a dark frown.

"Well, maybe you just thought it," she said gently with a smile and lifted her hand when she could see he was going to protest. "It doesn't matter. You'll soon see there's more to me than you thought. I'll be very happy in my cozy cottage."

"Okay," he said reluctantly. "As you wish. However, I insist on providing you with security. You'll have a guard within the next couple of days."

Ericka made a face. "If you insist," she said. "Just make sure whoever you choose is low-profile or they'll get on my nerves. No one too pushy."

"I do insist, and I'll make sure you have the best security possible. You're working for the palace, so protection is more than appropriate. The new rules specify that if any of the Devereaux family is working for Chantaine, they shall be given security. You're taking over the coordination for the conference for The Royal Society for A Better World, although I don't know how you expect to do it with a baby and no husband," he said.

"Single mothers have been accomplishing great things for ages," she said. "I'll have a nanny and two sisters willing to help."

"Along with Eve," Stefan said of his wife. "She would kill me if I didn't offer her assistance."

Ericka smiled still amazed at the change Eve had wrought in her brother. The two were soul mates. Her happiness faded a little when she thought of her own future romantic prognosis. She wasn't sure her soul mate existed. Brushing the thought aside, she knew it was silly for her to waste one moment on any ideas about romance. She had no time or energy for a man in her life right now.

"You're always welcome at the palace if you should change your mind."

"Thank you, but I won't," she said. "Now shall we cover a few issues about the upcoming conference?"

Stefan shot her a smile that held a hint of approval. "Down to business already?"

"I've been ready," she said, and powered up her tablet.

Two days later, Stefan sent Ericka a text message informing her that one of his assistants would be bringing her security detail to her for introduction. Ericka frowned at her phone in response. This wasn't the best time. She was tired and hadn't even taken a shower yet. Leo hadn't slept well and had been fussy throughout the night. Even though Nanny Marley was more than able to care for Leo, Ericka had wanted to soothe him. Ericka was finding it more difficult than she'd planned to turn Leo's care over to someone else.

Silly. Ericka had never considered herself overly nurturing, but Leo had provoked powerful changes within her. Of course now that sunlight streamed through the windows of the cottage, Leo slept peacefully.

Yawning, she pulled her hair into a topknot and quickly changed clothes. She dashed to the bathroom to splash water on her face and brush her teeth. The introduction with her security detail shouldn't take any longer than five minutes. After that, she planned to sneak in a little nap before working. Before Leo, Ericka would never have considered meeting someone without being turned out to as close to perfection as possible. Having a baby had changed her priorities.

A knock sounded at the door and she rushed to answer it. Leo was already being treated for his hearing disability with infant hearing aids, and Ericka never knew what sounds might awaken him.

Spotting her brother's assistant through the glass

window beside the door, she opened it. She immediately caught sight of a man standing just behind
her brother's assistant. He stood at least as tall as her
brother-in-law from Texas. Over six feet tall. How
was this subtle? she wondered. He would stick out
like a sore thumb in Chantaine. What had her brother
been thinking?

"Hello, Your Highness. Rolf here," her brother's
assistant said as he made a quick bow. "I'm here to
introduce you to your primary security detail. Mr.
Montreat Walker."

Ericka nodded toward Rolf then turned to Mr.
Walker out of politeness. "Mr. Walker."

He gave a half-hearted dip of his head. "You can
call me Treat," he said in a Texas twang.

"Oh, really," she said, thinking he was not a treat.
With his stubborn chin and too-broad shoulders, he
looked as if he would be a pain in her derriere. "Mr.
Walker," she said then turned to Rolf, who appeared
to be cowering from both her and Mr. *Treat* Walker.
"Thank you so much for stopping by. I'll be in touch
with Stefan."

"I'd like to check your home security system
first," Mr. Walker said.

"Excuse me," she replied, unable to hide her dis-
approval.

"Yes," the overly tall, overly muscular, overly
American man, said. "I've been hired to protect you.
I need to make sure your home is adequately secure."

"I have a security system," she told him.

"Then you won't mind me checking it," he said.

Actually, she would, but she couldn't say that. She shrugged and opened her door widely. "Don't wake my baby."

He lifted his eyebrows for a half-beat then stepped forward. "I'll do the best I can, but I will need to test your alarm system."

Ericka stared at Rolf. "Please tell my brother I'll be in touch," she said.

"Yes, Your Highness," he said before he dipped his head and walked away.

"I'm a done deal," Mr. Walker said to her. "Your brother has made his decision."

Ericka tried to look down her nose at him, but he was too darn tall. "Nothing is a done deal."

Mr. Walker shrugged. "Good luck. I'll check your system."

Ericka frowned at him as he swaggered through the hallway. "I told you not to wake my baby."

Mr. Walker paused and turned to look at her. "How strong is his hearing disorder?"

Ericka could have cried at his question. If only she knew how extensive his hearing loss was. Even the doctors had told her the measurement for his hearing disorder could change. "Profound. He's been awake most of the night."

Mr. Walker nodded. "I'll check the house. I'll have

to test the alarm system some time. You let me know when I can do that without startling him."

If only he *could* startle Leo, Ericka thought. If only she could make a sound that would startle him. Ericka stared after Mr. Walker, hating him and liking him at the same time. What could he possibly know about having a child with special needs? Nothing, she suspected. His life had probably been perfect. No troubles. No trials.

Leo's future was full of trials. She stiffened her back. She needed to cushion her child in his infancy and make him strong for his future years. Her job was to provide the perfect amount of support and hope. Whatever that was.

A flash of fur passed between them.

Mr. Walker frowned. "Was that a cat?"

"Yes. The doctor said Leo would benefit from a pet."

He frowned in confusion. "A cat? Don't they sleep twenty-three out of twenty-four hours a day?"

"Sam is awake much more than that, plus he watches after Leo."

"You mean, he stalks your baby," Mr. Walker said.

She blinked. "He does no such thing. Sam protects Leo. He's probably studying you right now to make sure you won't hurt the baby."

Mr. Walker lifted a dark eyebrow. "This is one more challenge for implementing a sound security system."

She lifted her head. "Sam stays. We brought him back from Texas. My brother insisted he was neutered before we arrived. Stefan doesn't want any more potent cats on the island. He's afraid Chantaine will end up with too many cats."

"Understandable," Mr. Walker said. "Practical."

"Mr. Walker, you need to understand that you're dealing with a very human element. My son. I know that the people of Chantaine don't hold a grudge against me. They're delighted I have returned."

"But there could be one person who's not delighted," he said. "And I'm here to protect you from that person."

Ericka stared into his dark eyes and knew he would protect her from anything. She held his gaze for a long moment and saw a flash of tenderness. It surprised her. How could a man who appeared so hard be kind?

If he couldn't be kind to her son, she had no use for him. If he couldn't tolerate her cat, he would be dismissed.

Treat Walker looked into Princess Fredericka's disapproving blue eyes. He'd read her file. She'd been known as the teenage wild-child beauty. She'd even made a few trips to rehab before she'd gotten herself straightened out and married a French film director.

Although the princess had returned to Chantaine frequently for public and family events, she'd seemed to prefer life out of the limelight. With the exception of red carpet appearances with her husband, Fredericka had focused more of her time on studies in fine arts.

When her husband fell for a younger actress, Fredericka's life began to fall apart. The combination of the scandal and her pregnancy had been overwhelming, so she'd disappeared to live in Texas with her older sister during her pregnancy.

At first glance, she looked a little too perfect. With her aristocratic bone structure, she could have modeled for a Renaissance sculptor. Although she was trying to hold him in cool contempt, he glimpsed humanity and a little bit of fear in her eyes, a hint of purple shadows that showed she wasn't sleeping well.

Taking care of an infant with serious hearing loss could be hard on anyone, especially since she appeared to be trying to do most of it on her own. "Your son," he said. "He's lucky you have the resources to give him the best help he needs. Not everyone can get their child the right kind of help."

Her eyebrows knitted slightly. "Money can't solve everything. The choices may be difficult," she said before she turned away from him.

Ericka spent the day juggling caring for Leo and planning her work schedule. Since the nanny had gone to market, Ericka carried Leo in a cloth baby carrier against her chest as she talked on the phone.

Leo quickly drifted off to sleep and Ericka answered a few calls. When he began to drool against her collar, she suspected he was ready for genuine nap in his crib. Just as she pulled him from the cloth carrier and set him in his crib, he let out a squeak of protest.

Wincing, Ericka immediately placed her hand over his tummy. Her sister had taught her this trick. Leo didn't like the abruptness of being detached after being held. A little more of a human connection seemed to soothe him and he gave a little snorty baby sigh. Ericka held her hand on him for several more moments, staring at his rosy, plump cheeks and dark eyelashes against his perfect skin. Pride and love welled up inside her. He was the most beautiful thing she'd ever seen in her life.

Carefully backing away, Ericka turned around and pulled the door partway closed behind her. Then she walked straight into a wall. Or, it felt like a wall until it swore under its breath. Her heart hammering in panic, she opened her mouth to scream at the same time she looked up into the hard face of Mr. Walker.

She slumped in relief and he immediately clasped her arms as if he thought she were going to faint. The notion annoyed her, "Remove your hands from me," she said in the icy tone she'd learned from one of her governesses.

He immediately released her and she stumbled backward, glaring at me. "I thought you had left to get an alarm system. What are you doing here now? And why didn't you knock?"

"First, since I'm your security detail, I'm like a member of the family. I don't have to knock," he said.

"Oh, yes, you do," she said. "You're not family. You're staff. All staff knocks before entering."

"Plus I didn't want to wake your baby if he was sleeping," he continued.

She opened her mouth then closed it, feeling as if someone had let the air out of her balloon. "Well," she said, desperate to establish some boundaries with this man who seemed to take up entirely too much space. "You shouldn't come up behind me like that and startle me. There's no excuse for that."

"I was examining the hallway for the best alarm system."

He was so implacable, she thought, her irritation growing. "I'm not sure this is going to work," she said, and walked past him. "My nanny and I are working perfectly well together. Your presence is disruptive."

"Give me a couple days," he said. "You'll barely notice I'm around."

That did it, she thought. Mr. Walker was going back to the States. She would talk with Stefan that afternoon.

Except Stefan wasn't picking up his private cell phone, and his assistant said he was indisposed. Stalling tactics. Ericka recognized them because he'd used them before on rare occasions when he wanted things his way. She considered calling Stefan's wife, Eve, but with two young children and another on the way, Eve had her hands full. Besides, this was between her and Stefan.

Ericka made another call. "Bernard, this is Ericka again. How are you?"

"Quite well, Your Highness."

"I realize Stefan is quite busy today," she said.

"Yes, yes, he is," Bernard said.

"Lots of activity in his palace office," she said.

"It's often busy in the Prince's office. As you know, he works hard for the people of Chantaine."

"Of course he does. Since he is at the Palace office today, I'll just scoot over for a quick visit. I promise it won't take more than a moment or two. Ciao," she said.

"But, but, but—"

Ericka disconnected the call and smiled grimly to herself. Two could play this little game. Stefan would be hard-pressed to avoid her if she was standing outside his office.

Ericka found Nanny Marley taking a well-earned break reading in the sunroom. "Marley, I need to make a quick trip to the palace. I won't be gone long."

"Yes, Your Highness. I'll keep an ear out for him."

Ericka shook her finger at the sweet middle-aged woman. "We've already discussed this. You're not supposed to address me as 'Your Highness.' Please call me Ericka."

"I keep forgetting," the woman said. "It just doesn't feel respectful."

"It's my wish," Ericka said. "So that makes it respectful. Please?"

"Yes, Miss Ericka," Nanny Marley said.

Ericka smiled. "That's a little closer. I'll be back soon."

"No hurries on my account, ma'am," the nanny said.

Ericka drove her tiny smart car through the winding streets of Chantaine. Her route to the palace took her past the view of the azure ocean trickling against a white sandy beach. She'd never realized how much she'd missed her homeland until she'd returned. In fact, she'd fought the idea of ever returning. She'd had too many memories of feeling confined and suffocated in Chantaine. Leaving had felt so freeing.

Even now, she felt twinges from her memories, but she was determined to keep her feelings and future in perspective. One of her most important decisions had been not to live at the palace. Another important decision had been to hire Nanny Marley. The next decision would be to get rid of her assigned security man, Mr. Walker.

As she pulled up to the palace, the gates were opened and she was waved through. Parking her car at the side of the main building, she touched her finger to the sensor that would allow her inside the door. Her shoes echoed on the marble floor of the hallways as she made her way to her brother's office. The same office had once belonged to her father, although her father had spent far less time performing royal duties and much more time on his yacht with his mistress du jour. She'd always found it amazing that her father had managed to sire six legitimate children despite his numerous affairs. Now that Ericka was grown, she could look back and see that her mother had continued to have children in hopes of truly winning her father's heart. Unfortunately, her mother's wish had never come true.

Ericka's stomach knotted as she remembered feeling that same sense of desperation at losing her husband. She'd been all too aware of the deterioration of his feelings for her. In fact, she'd made love with him in a final effort to win him back. When she thought of how weak she'd been, she could hardly bear it. It had taken her over a year to find herself again and get centered. She never wanted to be that weak woman, dependent on a man again. Never.

Reaching her brother's office, she knocked on the door and waited. Impatience nicked at her and she knocked again.

The door swung open and one of her brother's assistants dipped his head. "Your Highness," he said.

"I need to see my brother," she said.

"But he's—"

"It won't take long. I promise. Stefan," she called. "I know you're in there. Do you really want me yelling outside your office?"

Her brother's assistant groaned and seconds later, he backed away, allowing her entrance. Stefan frowned at her. "I just got off a conference call with two dukes from Spain and Italy."

"Great timing," she said, and shot him a broad smile. "I thought you might be signing off around this time."

"I actually had some other items on my list," he said, his irritation clear.

"I imagine they could wait until tomorrow. Eve and your little ones would probably love to see you tonight."

His hard gaze softened. "You're probably right. Eve is worn out by the end of the day with this pregnancy, although she would deny it."

"You married a strong woman," she said.

"So I did," Stefan said. "I suspect you're here to complain about your new security man."

"Your suspicion is correct. I specifically requested someone low key, who won't interrupt my routine or bring undue attention."

"Mr. Jackson will work out with no problem. He comes highly recommended. I wanted the best for you and Leo."

"You gave me the Texas version of the Jolly Green

Giant. He's been an interruption since he walked through the door. He doesn't like the cat—"

"Can't blame him there," Stefan muttered.

"Leo likes the cat," she said.

"Leo doesn't know any better," Stefan retorted. "Listen, you haven't even given Mr. Walker a chance. He hasn't been there a whole day. The least you can do is give him a trial period."

"One more day," she said.

Stefan shook his head. "At least a week. He left an assignment in the States at my request."

"I don't need this kind of invasion into my privacy. I can't believe you think Leo or I are at risk here in Chantaine."

"You forget Eve's encounter with that crowd before we were married," he said.

"That's different. I won't be doing nearly as many appearances since I'm focusing on the conference. Any time I'm making an appearance, you can assign someone from your security detail for me."

Stefan sighed. "I don't like to frighten you, but I don't trust your ex-husband. How do you know he won't try to use Leo to get some sort of settlement?"

Ericka's blood ran cold at the thought. She swallowed over a lump of fear and shook it off. "My ex-husband couldn't be less interested in Leo. He knew I was pregnant when I left."

"He could change his mind. If he does, I want to be ready for him."

Chapter Two

Treat heard two voices coming from the den of the house as he walked down the hall. He stopped outside the den and watched as the princess used sign language while she gazed at her computer tablet. The baby sat next to her with his eyes closed, apparently asleep.

"So, how did you like that, Leo?" she asked and turned to look at her child. She gave a soft laugh. "Bored you to sleep, right?"

She sighed. "Well, maybe we can get you to extend your little nap in your crib," she said as she gently picked up the baby and stood. She turned and met his gaze.

Treat saw the way her body stiffened slightly.

"Anything I can do for you? I've decided to focus security around the perimeter of the property and give you and your nanny a panic button."

"Fine," she said with a total lack of interest. "I'm going to try to put Leo down now. He has a hard time sleeping unless he can see me or I'm holding him."

"Maybe it has something to do with his other senses being heightened. Do you leave a light on in the bedroom?" he asked.

"No. I hadn't thought of that," she said. "I use room darkening shades for him during the day."

Treat shrugged. "Just something to think about. He's probably a very visual guy."

She studied him for a moment. "I'll do some research."

He nodded. "Looked like you were doing well with the sign language," he said.

"You know sign language?" she asked.

"A little. Not enough to get any—" he said, and wiggled his hands for the sign for applause.

Her lips twitched in an almost smile. "I've got a long way to go. Right now, though, I'm putting my big guy to bed. I'm glad you won't be concentrating as much on alarming the house. Leo may not be able to hear the alarms, but it would be startling for Nanny and me."

"I hear you," he said. "Listen, do you mind if I take a swim in the pool at night? It's one of the ways I like to stay in shape."

He felt her gaze dip to his shoulders then she blinked and cleared her throat. "Of course not," she said. "Excuse me while I put Leo to bed."

Treat felt something wrap around his ankles and watched Sam wind around him. He frowned.

"Looks like Sam likes you," Princess Fredericka said.

Treat watched her as she retreated down the hall-way. He shifted from one foot to the other and narrowed his eyes. Sam looked up at him and gave a meow. He glared down at the cat, but the cat continued to mark him. Glancing toward the hallway, he thought about the woman who'd just left the room. He'd expected a snooty princess. At first glance, maybe she was. But in less than twenty-four hours, he'd glimpsed something else. A princess trying to teach herself and her baby son sign language? She wasn't what he'd expected.

Treat felt a strange gnawing sensation in his gut. He hadn't felt anything like it in a long time. In fact, he hadn't felt much of anything for a long time. He'd made sure not to invest in anything too emotional. His life hadn't allowed for it once he'd suffered that last professional football injury. Treat hadn't gotten truly involved with a woman in several years. He'd been too busy trying to make a living. Once he'd switched to security, he'd decided to make his fortune with it. The past few years he'd worked nonstop with his partner to build their security business.

Now, he was making the step to take the business international.

He needed cooperation from Princess Fredericka and he also needed not to get emotionally involved. No problem, he told himself.

Another near-sleepless night, Ericka thought as she rubbed her face when the sun shone through the crack of her window coverings. She wasn't sure when Leo had fallen asleep for more than an hour, but she planned to check out night lights and anything else that might help him. She'd finally turned on a lamp in the hallway. She wondered if that had helped.

Nanny was more than ready to step up, but Ericka had a hard time handing over Leo's care when he seemed so distressed. Now, however, she had calls and plans to make and she wouldn't feel quite so guilty handing Leo over to his nanny. Ericka was so exhausted that she knew she needed help.

Lying on her back in her bed, she took several deep breaths and stared up at the ceiling. She needed to open the blinds, she told herself. She'd recently read that exposure to light during the first thirty minutes of her day would make her feel more awake.

"Wake up, Ericka," she urged herself and dragged herself from her bed. She thrust herself under a shower, brushed her teeth then stumbled toward the kitchen where Nanny sat at the table.

"You should have woken me. That's why I'm here," she said, offering Ericka a cup of coffee.

"He was just on the edge," Ericka said, accepting the coffee and taking a long draw. "He kept going to sleep and waking up. Then going to sleep and waking up."

"You should have awakened me after the first time," Nanny said.

"I think it became a challenge," Ericka said.

"Oh," Nanny said in a dark voice. "That's bad. No one should ever challenge a Devereaux."

Ericka laughed and took another long drink from her coffee. "You're so right." She paused a half beat. "The security man suggested I do something with light to help Leo. Something about his sight being a strong sense. So I'm going to do some research."

"This from the American?"

Ericka nodded. "Who knew?"

Nanny shook her head. "I would not have expected that."

"Neither would I have," Ericka said.

Nanny lifted her hands in the sign language for applause. "Good for you. Good for Leo."

Ericka smiled and echoed the sign language. "We're working on it," she said. "In the meantime, it's time for me to go to work."

"Drink another cup of coffee," Nanny said.

Ericka extended her mug up toward the woman, who refilled her cup. "I'm so glad I don't have to meet face-to-face with anyone today. Thank good-ness this is a phone day."

"Take a nap midday then have juice and a cookie," Nanny said. "It will be good for you."

Ericka chuckled, but she couldn't help thinking Nanny had a good point. Maybe, if everyone took a nap after lunch followed by a snack of juice and a cookie, then the world would be a better place. She would be less cranky. That was for sure.

She made several calls throughout the day. Coffee kept her going. Just before dinner, she signed off and typed some final notes on her laptop. The confer-ence planning was coming along. She was pleased with her progress.

Ericka stood and shook her body to release her stiffness and tension. A short dip in the pool would do her good, she thought, and she went to her bed-room to change into a bathing suit. It was dinner time, but she was more interested in the sensation of sinking into water than eating. Thank goodness the pool was heated.

Ericka stepped down the stairs into the pool, paus-ing before the last step. The water was cooler than she'd expected. She finally took that last step and let out a little squeal. Sinking down to her neck, she shivered, but quickly adjusted.

She took a deep breath then plunged her face in the water and began to swim. She made it to the far wall and turned then swam back. Out of breath, she paused and chastised herself. "Go," she muttered to herself and swam another lap. She returned and grasped the side of the pool, gasping for air.

A warm hand covered hers on the side of the pool. "Are you okay?"

Surprised, she inhaled water and coughed. And coughed. And coughed. She felt a splash beside her and a thump on her back. She hacked a couple more times then took a low, careful breath through her nostrils.

"Did you have to startle me?" she finally managed, looking up at Mr. Walker who was fully dressed in jeans and a polo shirt. Drenched, he stared down at her, his shirt clinging to his perfectly muscled body.

"I thought you were drowning," he said. "You kept gasping for air but ducking your head under the water."

"I was pushing myself to go a little farther. I realize it may look pathetic in your eyes, but I haven't had a lot of physical exercise during the last few months."

"Oh," he said, watching her as she continued to catch her breath.

"Have you ever had a baby?" she asked.

His mouth twitched in a cockeyed smile. "Not that I can remember."

Ericka took a deep breath and headed toward the

steps. She felt his hands on her waist guiding her. "That's not—"

"No problem," he said, continuing to help her up the steps.

Her heart raced at his touch and she didn't like the sensation. "Let go of me. I'm fine."

He didn't release her until she was steady. She resented the fact that she wasn't steady one minute earlier. She resented him, too.

"I was just taking a swim," she said.

He stepped up beside her in his wet street cloths and looked down at her. "Maybe you shouldn't do as many laps next time."

"I didn't do that many," she retorted.

"Cut yourself some slack. Isn't your baby still waking up every night?" he asked.

"Yes," she said.

"And you don't let the nanny take over nearly often enough, then," he said.

Ericka took another deep breath, hating that he was speaking the truth. She so wanted him to be wrong. "I can handle it."

"I'm your security detail," he said, and extended his hand. "I can't let you drown yourself."

She ignored his hand and walked away, her limbs heavy from her exertion. "You ruined my swim."

"I saved you from drowning," he corrected.

She turned around and stared at him. "You are a total pain and you will be gone in six days."

He gave a crooked smile again. "Your brother insisted that you give me a trial period."

Ericka scowled. *I hate you*, she wanted to say. "Good night. You'll be gone soon enough," she said, and then turned to walk away.

"You know Beethoven wrote some of his most famous work when he was deaf," he said.

She stopped and her heart stopped, too. Ericka took a deep breath, more moved by his words than she would ever want to admit. "Good night," she repeated, although even she would admit she sounded less hostile.

Although she turned on a light in Leo's room, he still awakened in the middle of the night and screamed bloody murder. Nanny was there to help, but Ericka felt responsible. She was his mother. She was the one who should soothe him back to sleep. As soon as she drew him into her arms, he quieted.

As she rocked him in the middle of the night, she wondered if she would ever be the mother he needed. He was such a precious soul. How could she be all he needed?

She dozed a bit with him in her lap then rose and carefully placed him in the crib, keeping her hand on him for several moments. She felt him drift to sleep and carefully walked away.

An hour later, he awakened again. This time, she let Nanny take him. At the same time, she felt like a failure. Why couldn't she help her son so that he would sleep through the night?

Exhausted, she awakened later than usual and forced herself to climb out of bed. Stumbling toward the bath, she splashed her face with water and brushed her teeth then headed for the kitchen for coffee. She wanted to mainline it through her veins.

Nanny offered her a cup. "Would you like cream and sugar, ma'am?"

"That sounds wonderful," Ericka said. "Have you gotten any sleep since four am?"

"Yes, ma'am, I have," Nanny said. "His royal self gave it up after half a bottle. Men," she said, shaking her head. "It's all about food."

Ericka chuckled and took a sip of her coffee. "So true. And this morning?"

"He's still asleep," Nanny said.

"That can be good," Ericka said. "And bad."

Nanny nodded. "I'll take a nap in just a few moments," she said.

"I'm thinking of hiring back-up assistance for cooking and cleaning," Ericka said.

"It shouldn't be necessary," Nanny said. "I know our arrangement is for me to return to my apartment a few days every month. Is that a problem?" the woman asked with a worried expression.

"Not at all. Trust me, you are irreplaceable. I think a little additional back-up may help. For both of us,"

Ericka said. "Leo has us coming and going. There's too much of cooking and cleaning left to do."

"Well, it's not as if you're a woman of leisure," Nanny said. "You work very hard."

Ericka felt a sliver of relief. "Thank you for saying that. I somehow feel as if I should manage all of this on my own."

Nanny shook her head. "Never. It's not as if you have a husband," she said, and then covered her mouth as if she were shocked by her frank words.

Ericka shook her head. "Don't worry. What you say is true. I'm just trying to figure it all out."

"And you're doing a wonderful job," Nanny said. "Don't be so hard on yourself. It won't help you get any job done, motherhood or your other duties."

Ericka made more phone calls to continue to secure the arrangements for the upcoming conference. Her sister Bridget called in between calls. "Hello, Bridget, how are you?"

"Pregnant and busy with the twins and all the animals my husband insists on having at our so-called ranch. When I agreed to marry a Texan doctor, I didn't realize he was serious about recreating home on the range here in Chantaine," Bridget said in a mock huffy voice.

Ericka smiled at her sister's tone. Although Bridget had been known as the socialite in her family, she'd been tamed when she'd fallen in love with her doctor husband and the two nephews he'd adopted. "More animals? Horses, cattle, goats. You're turning into a zoo,"

"Oh, darling, we became a zoo a long time ago," she said. "Now, I know you're busy, but Pippa, Eve and I want to have a get-together for lunch before I get much closer to my due date. Before you know it, it will be Christmas. Or I'll be in labor. One of the two."

"I'd love to," Ericka said, "but I'm feeling strapped for time. Between caring for Leo and planning the conference…"

"I feel terrible that you've had to take over the conference, but when the doctor put me on limited activity, it squashed my schedule even more. You have a nanny and back-up, don't you?"

"I have a wonderful nanny, but I think I'm going to have to get someone part-time for shopping and errands," Ericka said.

Bridget made a tsk-ing sound. "You should have done that right away. Trying to do too much. You're starting to act like overachiever Valentina before her husband took her away from us."

Ericka smiled at the description. Bridget had nailed Tina's personality perfectly. "I'm not sure I'll ever measure up to those standards," Ericka said.

"Well, you have too much right now, so I think you should ask for a loaner or referral from the palace. Anyone they recommend will have been properly vetted. You can ask for a few choices," Bridget said.

"I've been trying to avoid placing any extra burdens on the palace," she confessed.

"Oh, yes. I know all about it. Stefan is huffing and puffing because you won't stay at the palace where he can make sure you're safe and secure. Can't blame you for wanting to escape, though. Even though I live in a circus with these five-year old twins and all these animals, I much prefer living outside the walls. But I insist you let the palace help you out. I also insist you join us for lunch day after tomorrow. No arguments," Bridget said in her best no-nonsense voice.

"All right," Ericka said. "When did you become so bossy?"

"You get a family of instant twin baby boys and you'll be amazed how bossy you become. Ciao, darling. Go eat some chocolate and have some wine. Drink an extra glass for me."

Although reluctant, Ericka put in a call to palace personnel. Two applicants would apply tomorrow. She fed the baby and carried him around for a while. Suddenly it was eight o'clock and she was tired and cranky. Thank goodness for Nanny. She thought about how Bridget had suggested wine and chocolate, but she was in the mood for something different. Something she'd had when she was pregnant and living in Texas.

A peanut butter and bacon sandwich.

* * *

Treat followed the scent of bacon inside the house. He'd missed that smell. "Bacon?" he said.

Ericka whirled around to look at him. "Technically pancetta."

"Smells like bacon," he said.

"It's not quite the same thing," she said. "But I'll make do. If I burn it enough and put it on top of peanut butter, it won't matter that much."

"Peanut butter?" he echoed, impressed by her determination.

She nodded and turned back to her frying pan. "My brother-in-law from Texas turned me onto this when I was pregnant. It has turned into one of my favorite stress foods."

She flipped the pancetta onto a paper towel while she slathered a slice of bread with a peanut butter.

"Hey," Treat said. "Do you have any extra bacon?"

"Pancetta," she corrected.

"It smells great," he said.

She chuckled. "Here you go."

"I think I want to try it with peanut butter," he said.

She slid him a sideways glance. "I don't have a lot of extra peanut butter," she said. "My sister from Texas sends it to me."

"Okay," Treat said. "I'll just take the bacon."

She gave a heavy sigh and pulled out two more slices of bread. Slapping some peanut butter on a slice, she followed with a helping of crispy pancetta and squished the sandwich together. She handed it to him on a plate. "Eat at your own risk."

"I'll brave it," he said, then took a big bite and savored the flavors. He took another bite to assess. "It's delicious. The pancetta's a little strong, but it's still delicious."

"Agreed," Ericka said. "I'm trying to figure out how to get American bacon, although I know I've just offended every Italian I've ever met."

"The pancetta's not bad," he said, taking another big bite of the sandwich.

"No, but I want cheap bacon," she said, and took a bite of her own sandwich.

"If anyone should be able to get it, you should," he said. "You're a princess."

"We have importation rules," she said, and continued to eat her sandwich. "I wonder if I talked to Stefan. Or if I kept my mouth shut and asked Tina to send me American bacon…"

"What a scandal that could be," he said. "Princess Fredericka imports forbidden bacon."

She slid a quelling glance at him, then chuckled. "I suppose you're right. I could be importing so much worse."

He swallowed the rest of his sandwich and nodded. He brushed off his hands. "So right. Time for bed?"

She met his gaze and choked on her sandwich.

Treat smacked her on her back. He wondered if he should perform the Heimlich.

Ericka coughed then stepped away from him. "I'm fine," she insisted, coughing.

"You sure?" he asked.

"Yes," she said, still coughing.

He poured a glass of water and offered it to her.

Ericka sipped it then took a shallow breath. "I think you're right. It's time to go to bed."

Treat nodded. "Let me know if you need me for anything."

"I'm fine, Mr. Walker," she said.

"Call me Treat," he said.

"Treat?" she echoed and shook her head. "What an interesting name."

"Montreat," he said. "The name was shortened."

"Oh," she said, and then nodded.

"Kinda like Fredericka was shortened to Ericka."

"Interesting," she said. "Mr. Walker. Good night."

"Good night, Princess Fredericka," he said.

"I need to clean up," she said.

"I can do that," he said. "Go on up to bed. You need your sleep."

She paused a moment. "If you insist, Mr. Walker."

"Treat," he corrected.

She paused a long moment. "Treat," she finally said in a soft voice. The sound of his name from her lips did something to him. He would have to figure that out later.

"Night," he said as he watched her leave the room. Treat cleaned the pan and dishes then prowled the kitchen. Fifteen minutes later, he heard the sound of Leo crying. He knew Ericka would get up and cradle her baby. He also knew she needed rest.

Treat climbed the stairs. He nearly bumped into Ericka.

"What are you doing here?" she whispered.

"I'm checking on your baby," he said.

"I can take care of that," she told him.

"But maybe you shouldn't," he said. "Even Saint Ericka needs a rest."

She scowled at him. "I've never said I'm a saint."

"Then stop trying to look like one," he said. "Go back to bed."

"Who will hold Leo?" she asked.

"I will," he said.

"You?" she asked. "You look like you would be better with a football."

"Football, baby, they're close to the same."

"A baby is close to a football?" she said, clearly alarmed.

"I'm joking," he said. "I've rocked a baby before. Trust me."

"Why should I?" she asked.

"Your brother did," he said. "He vetted me six times from Sunday."

Ericka sighed, clearly so weary she could hardly stand. "Just for a few minutes," she said. "Just a few minutes. Then wake me up. I can handle this." She turned toward her room and Treat felt a crazy quiet sense of victory as he entered the nursery and picked up the baby.

Chapter Three

Ericka awakened in the night and listened for sounds from the baby monitor. Nothing. She stared up at the ceiling then closed her eyes and told herself she should go back to sleep. Leo wasn't crying. All was well.

Except the football player was looking after her baby. Rising and pushing her covers aside, she shook her head at herself. She must have been out of her mind to put Leo in his care. Rushing to the nursery, she carefully pushed the door open and saw Treat moving the beam of a flashlight against the ceiling. He saw her and lifted his fingers to his lips to urge her to remain quiet.

Ericka looked at Leo whose sleepy gaze followed

the light. His eyelids drooped then opened then finally closed. She tilted her head and looked at Treat in silence. He placed the flashlight on the small dresser then stood and ushered her out of the room, gently closing the door behind them.

"What was that about?" she asked.

"I told you he might like more light," he said.

"That's why I put a nightlight in there," she said.

"I think he likes something more active. It's a challenge to track a moving light. He's a smart little guy," he said.

Ericka took in Treat's last words and it was all she could do not to burst into tears. Although she believed Leo was smart, she hadn't heard anyone else say those exact words. He'd been called beautiful and alert, but no one had called him smart. Ericka bit her lip, determined to pull her emotions in check. "Yes, he is smart," she said as she crossed her arms over her chest. "Thank you for looking after him. It's not really your job."

"I don't require a lot of sleep," he said.

"I envy you that," she muttered. Suddenly she realized how close he stood to her. She could smell the faint scent of soap and shampoo. He was so tall, she thought, and told herself she found that fact off-putting. She looked into his eyes and her stomach took a strange dip. *What was that?* She took a quick short breath and looked away. "You can go to bed.

Nanny and I should be able to handle it now. Thank you again."

"No problem," he said, and walked past her down the hallway to the front door. He slept in the small guest suite. Attached to the cottage, the suite had its own door. For a moment, she wondered what he did all day in that suite when he wasn't figuring out new ways to protect her and Leo. It occurred to her that all that solitary confinement would make her batty. Sure, she enjoyed quiet moments enjoying art. She especially missed those moments lately, but Ericka needed human connection. She wondered if Treat did.

Suddenly realizing she'd been thinking about him for at least three full moments, she shook her head and reminded herself that she didn't care if Treat needed human connection or not. She just wanted him to stay out of the way so she could do what she needed to do.

Treat returned to the guest suite but felt like a caged animal. He felt he shouldn't leave the property to go for a run, so he decided to take a swim. Maybe that would relax him. He slid into the pool and the water felt warm against his skin, probably because the night air was cool. Automatically swimming several laps, he waited for the exercise and the monotony of motion to ease his mind.

Being around the princess's baby brought back

memories of his disabled brother, Jerry. Jerry had been born with multiple deformities, both mental and physical, but he'd had a good soul. Treat had seen it in his young brother's eyes and smile.

Treat had noticed that Leo didn't smile as frequently. Leo looked as if he were trying to figure everything out. The baby appeared to want every bit of information he could get and he wanted it immediately. A demanding baby, he thought, and not just because of his hearing loss.

His brother, Jerry, had been demanding due to his health issues which had been enormous. After Treat's father died when he was a teenager, Treat had watched his mother struggle to pay medical bills. He had cared for Jerry whenever he could, but his mother had pushed him to take a football scholarship. It had always been Treat's dream to make a lot of money so that he could take care of both his mother and Jerry.

But Jerry had died during Treat's junior year in college and he'd lost his mother just one year later. She hadn't even seen Treat graduate. Treat had felt like a rudderless boat after that.

Even though he knew the princess's situation was far different than his mother's, he caught glimpses of the same emotions he'd seen in his mother's eyes. Fear, worry, weariness. He also saw a helluva lot of determination. Ericka would make sure Leo received every bit of education and attention he needed. She could have taken an easier way out, but he could tell she would be actively involved in every decision in that baby's life. Leo was damn lucky, not just because his mother was a princess, but because she was so devoted.

Treat swam a few more laps. The vision of the princess and Leo stomped through his mind. Swimming hadn't extricated them from his consciousness, but maybe the exercise would help him sleep. Her Highness was making a bigger impact on him than he'd expected.

Ericka rose early and conducted two teleconferences. She much preferred regular phone calls because for those, she didn't need to apply make-up or fix her hair. During another call later in the morning, she received the disturbing news that young royals from Sergenia were in danger and needed to leave their small country due to unrest.

Ericka turned off her phone and did a session with Leo. She showed him several works of art and signed the best she could. "Here is da Vinci's Mona Lisa," she said, lifting her computer tablet. "He was a brilliant artist. As was Raphael." She pulled up a photo of one of Raphael's paintings. "I can't wait to show you Michelangelo's sculpture of David," she told her son. "It's beyond amazing. There's nothing like it," she said, and waved the hand toward her face making the sign for amazing.

"I must have been way behind," Treat said from the doorway. "I didn't know anything about da Vinci until I was in my teens. Unless you count the Teenage Mutant Ninja Turtles."

"Who are they?" she asked, feeling a strange rush of pleasure when she saw him.

"Cartoon turtle characters named after some of the great artists of the Renaissance," he said. "Michelangelo, Raphael, Donatello and Leonardo."

"How clever," she said.

He chuckled. "You learned about the real artists. I learned about the cartoon characters."

Ericka frowned in sympathy. "How unfortunate," she said.

He chuckled again. "No worries. I received a little more education later on and saw pictures of the Renaissance artists. I'm okay. Just not as cultured as you are."

Ericka met his gaze and felt her stomach jump. "You can learn."

"I do my best. Are you ready to go out for your luncheon with your sisters?"

"Yes" she said, standing as she remembered. "Nanny will take care of Leo."

"I'm sure he's exhausted from his morning lecture," he said.

She narrowed her eyes at him. "Are you saying I'm boring him?"

Treat lifted his hands. "Not me."

"I need to freshen up," she said. "I'll be back in a moment. Nanny Marley," she called and walked down the hall.

Treat walked over to look at Leo. "How ya doing big guy? Wanna talk football?"

Leo kicked and stared at him, making grunting sounds.

"Just so you know, Bonnie Sloan was one of the first deaf NFL football players. You can do anything you want," Treat said. "When you get a little older, maybe we can toss the pigskin."

A half-beat later, Nanny Marley entered the room. "How's he doing?"

"He's just received a very cultural tutoring session," Treat said.

Nanny nodded and smiled. "Her Highness is highly motivated to expose Leo to art, culture and science."

"What about sports?" he asked.

"That may be someone else's job," Nanny said.

Princess Fredericka strode into the hallway. "Ready," she said, and quickly ran to Leo to give him a kiss on his chubby cheek.

"Yes, Your Highness," Treat said, and walked with her out of the house.

"You don't have to call me 'Your Highness,'" she said.

"Oh, really," he said. "Then what do I call you?"

"For the remainder of your service, you may call

me Ericka in private," she said as she walked to the car.

"And what do I call you in public?" he asked.

"Miss," she said. "Just call me Miss."

"Done and done, Ericka," he said as he helped her into the car.

Just a few moments later, Treat drove to the café where Ericka planned to meet her sisters and sister-in-law. Although she was more than willing to hop out as he approached the curb, he refused to let her out. "I'll escort you into the café," he said.

"Well, don't expect to stay," she told him as he parked the car. "There will already be security for the rest of the crowd. You'll be superfluous."

"Superfluous," he echoed as he walked her into the café.

She gave a heavy sigh. "It's not an attack against your masculinity. When it comes to security, my brother Stefan provides overkill."

"I'm glad he's protective. You are all valuable to him and many others," Treat said. "There's your table. I'll be outside. Call me if you need me."

Ericka was still contemplating his statement about how valuable she and her sisters were, but Bridget stood, in her immense pregnancy, and extended her arms.

"Ericka, come here and give me a big hug. I need it. Maybe you can squeeze away some of my swelling," Bridget said.

Ericka smiled and rushed toward her sister and gave Bridget a hug as big as her pregnancy. "So good to see you. You look great."

"I'll look so much better in a few weeks. Look at Eve. She's doing fabulously. Six months pregnant and she looks like she could deliver after a full day of plowing fields."

"I hope not," Eve said, kissing Ericka on the cheek. "How's our little boy Leo?"

"Wonderful when he sleeps," Ericka said. "Which doesn't seem to happen at night."

"Oh, no," Pippa, Ericka's other sister said. "Hopefully, he'll sleep soon."

Ericka felt Pippa search her face and wished she could hide her emotions.

"You should call me for help," Pippa said.

"You're busy with your own baby," Ericka said.

"Not too busy for family. Any news on treatment?" Pippa asked.

"We're still working with hearing aids, but we haven't seen any improvement. Surgery may be in his future, but I want to make sure he's ready for it. Even with surgery, I'll teach him sign language. Of course, I'm learning it, too."

"You know the rest of us will be right there with you," she said. "We're happy to learn sign language. It would be good for the children. It would be good for all of us."

Ericka's heart swelled and she felt her eyes fill

with tears. "You're so sweet," she said, embracing Pippa. "So very sweet."

"Oh, stop," Pippa said. "Let's have a nice holiday lunch."

Ericka sat down with her sisters and sister-in-law and enjoyed a non-alcoholic cranberry spritzer along with a salad then a chicken crepe. Afterward, the women enjoyed chocolate mousse pie.

"Delicious," Bridget said.

"I agree," Ericka said.

"Stefan says you're doing a great job with the royal society conference," Bridget said.

Eve nodded. "He said the same to me."

"And me," Pippa added.

Ericka felt her cheeks heat with self-consciousness. "Thanks. Our colleagues have been very responsive."

"Good to hear," Eve said.

"I did receive an unsettling call this morning. You know that Sergenia is experiencing some unrest and the princesses and prince need a place to go. I think Chantaine would be perfect."

"But we're such a small country. How could they possibly hide here?" Pippa asked.

"Different identities and jobs." Ericka said. "They're amenable to such a plan."

"But would Stefan agree?" Bridget asked. "He has always wanted to remain neutral."

"Perhaps with the proper pressure," Ericka said, then glanced at Eve. "I hate to ask you."

"Give me more details later and I'll see what I can do. He's a stubborn, but wonderful, man," Eve said. "That's why we all love him."

"True," Pippa murmured then lifted her glass of soda. "To good health, happiness and the future of the Devereaux family."

"Here, here," Eve said. Bridget echoed the cheer as did Ericka.

"And next week, we meet publicly for the lighting of the royal Christmas tree," Eve said. "Bridget excused."

"If I can be there, I will," Bridget said, and then took another sip of her cranberry beverage. "In the meantime, we've just added a couple new goats to our zoo. Too many in my opinion. Do any of you want a goat?"

Silence followed. No takers. Ericka nearly choked over her spritzer, but she swallowed hard to quell the urge so that Bridget wouldn't mistake any sound she made as interest in taking on one of her goats.

After hugs all around, the women headed out the door. Ericka waited for her sisters and sister-in-law to leave then strode outside. A crowd awaited her, taking her by surprise.

"Hello," she managed and Treat appeared by her side.

Several people rushed toward her and Treat stepped in front of her. "Go to the car," he instructed her. "It's behind you."

Ericka rushed into the vehicle and Treat followed, driving her away from the crowd. "Next time, you won't leave last," he said sternly. "The crowd caught on after your sisters left."

"I was merely being polite," she protested.

"Next time you'll leave at the same time they leave or before," he said. "Think about it. If I hadn't been there, you could have been crushed."

She wanted to argue, but she knew he was right. She had underestimated how much the people wanted to connect with the royals. Now that she was a mother, she had to think more carefully about her safety. Thank goodness Treat had been there to protect her.

As he drove into her gated cottage, she felt a sense of safety settle over her. He helped her out of the car. "Thank you," she said quietly. "I was so busy fighting for my independence that I didn't realize I was sacrificing security." She looked into his gaze and noticed a scrape and a trickle of blood on his forehead. "You were hurt."

He shook his head. "Someone just got a little pushy."

Horrified, she lifted her hand. "I'm so sorry. We need to bandage it," she said.

"It's no big deal," he said. "Trust me. I've suffered much worse. Are you okay?"

"Me?" she echoed. "I'm fine. You took care of me."

"Good," he said. "Go inside. Take a break or a

nap. I'll be in the guest room unless you want to go anywhere."

"Of course," she said, standing on the porch as he walked away, wanting to put a bandage on his wound.

She felt a bit stupid after fighting her brother and Treat. As much as she wanted to think she could walk around like anyone else, she just couldn't. And she needed to face that fact for both herself and Leo.

The next day, the artificial pre-lit Christmas arrived outside her well-secured gate. Treat brought it inside. "Good news. There are only three pieces."

She looked at the mark on his forehead and pressed her lips together in concern.

"Stop staring at my little mark," he said, waving his hand in her face. "We need to get this tree put up for Leo. Where is the little sleep-stealer, anyway?"

"I hate to wake him," she said.

Treat dropped his chin and shook his head. "Well, he sure doesn't mind waking you. Besides, this will be a great visual experience for him."

"You're right," she said, clapping her hands as she strode toward the nursery and went against every motherly instinct by waking him. His sweet little eyebrows frowned as she lifted him from his crib.

"Trust me," she said. "You're gonna love this." Ericka was determined to continue talking to Leo even though he couldn't hear a word she was saying. In a few months, if he got the surgery, he would be able to hear her, so she needed to keep talking to him. Shifting him slightly, she grabbed his infant seat and walked to the den. "We're ready," she said as she set Leo into his seat.

"All right, all right," Treat said. "Let's rock and roll."

In a stunningly short amount of time, he put the tree up. Leo squirmed and sucked on his pacifier, but didn't cry.

Treat plugged in the lights and Leo stopped squirming and sucking, gaping at the lights.

"He loves it," Ericka said, delighted. "He loves the lights."

Treat smiled and nodded. "Bet he'll love it even more after we put on the ornaments."

"Oh," she said. "In the top of my closet in my bedroom. My sister gave them to me. I'll get them."

"No," he said. "You stay here. I'll get them."

Ericka turned to Leo and cooed. "You like the lights, don't you? Christmas is a wonderful time of love and hope, Leo," she said to her sweet infant son. "Never ever forget that."

Treat returned with the two boxes of ornaments and garland. "I hope you have some ornament hangers."

'I'm sure Valentina included them. We just need to find them," she said, and opened the boxes. It took only a few seconds to locate the hangers. "Here they are."

"Let's get moving, then. Garland first," he said as he began to spread the garland around the tree.

Ericka helped adjust the greenery. A half beat later, he grabbed a handful of hangers. Before she knew it, he hung five ornaments.

"Wait a minute," she muttered and began to hang silver and red balls. "You seem quite experienced at this."

"I was usually assigned the job of setting of the Christmas tree and decorating it," he said.

"Did you set a speed record?" she asked, hanging more ornaments.

"I wanted the tree decorated and then I wanted out of the house," he said, adding five more ornaments in no time at all.

"Why?" she asked, searching his gaze. "Why did you want out of your house?"

He shrugged as he hung the ornaments. "It wasn't all silver bells and gingerbread at my house," he said. "But that tree was good for everyone and I liked seeing it every time I came into the house. It was sad when we took it down on New Year's Day."

Ericka nodded. "I don't remember putting up the tree or taking it down. The rest of the palace felt cold. I remember wishing I could sleep under the tree, but, of course that wasn't possible. Last year, I spent Christmas with my sister in Texas. It was a totally different experience. I want to give that to Leo."

"You are," Treat said, and hung several more ornaments.

Within five minutes, they had mostly finished decorating.

Treat stepped away and gazed at the tree in approval. "Looks good."

Leo gave a high-pitched squeal of delight.

Ericka looked at her son then at Treat. "That's a first," she said.

"Well, it's his first Christmas. I'm gonna take that as a thumbs up. If he was looking at a Picasso, I might interpret it differently."

Ericka shook her head and laughed. His comment gave her a wonderful, surprising sense of lightness that she'd rarely experienced since she'd given birth to Leo. Everything felt so serious, so important. So dire.

She looked at Leo and he smiled and laughed. Joy filled her, starting in her belly and shooting up to her chest, throat and cheeks. She laughed again, staring at Leo and savoring his joy.

The moment was delightful and sacred. She couldn't have explained it in any language, but she was so glad she'd brought Leo to Chantaine and decided to have Christmas in this cottage. Her heart was so full that her eyes burned with tears.

"Thank you," she said, then began to repeat it in

every language she knew. *"Grazie, Merci, Gracias, Danke..."*

He put his finger over her mouth. "I get it," he said. "You're welcome." He looked at Leo and grinned. "You're very welcome."

Ericka sucked in a teeny tiny breath into her tight chest and nodded.

"I need to check the perimeter," he said, and met her gaze. "You've done well."

"Me?" she squeaked. "You're the one who put this together in no time."

"Don't underestimate yourself. Or Leo," he said, and walked away.

She watched him leave, then she burst into tears and stroked Leo's face as he stared at the Christmas tree in wonder.

That night, Treat did his job and he made sure the house was secure. He made sure the princess and Leo were secure. He stayed away from his precious charges but watched over them.

Grabbing a sandwich, he ate it then took a swim. He swam several laps and the water felt good over his body. Finally, he stopped and hung over the edge of the pool. He took several deep breaths to clear his head.

Images of Leo swam through his brain. The princess permeated his mind. Treat shook his head and swam several more laps. He was caught between driving himself to the point where he was forced to sleep and the point where he had to stay awake to take care of the princess and Leo.

Chapter Four

The cat greeted Treat as he entered the den the next morning, and he immediately realized that he needed to secure the tree. He raced to his room to retrieve twine then returned to the den.

"What are you doing? Why are you running around?" Princess Fredericka asked, appearing in the doorway, her hair mussed from sleep as she pulled a light robe around her.

"Because I need to secure this tree," he said. "I should have done it yesterday."

"Why?" she asked, clearly bemused.

"Because you have a cat," he said. "And cats love to tear up Christmas trees."

"Oh," she said, her sexy, sweet lips forming a perfect O.

Treat scanned the floor to make sure Sam hadn't already grabbed a few ornaments. Then he wrapped twine around the tree and tied it around a vent plug. He wrapped more twine around the tree and a chair leg. He wasn't all that happy with that choice, but he figured it was better than nothing.

Treat decided to place a nail in the wall and wrap yet another bit of twine around it.

"You think that's enough?" she asked.

"I hope so," he said. "But cats are clever and destructive."

"Sam won't be destructive. He's very sweet."

"How long have you had a cat?" he asked.

"Three months here. Longer in Texas," she said.

"How much longer in Texas?" he asked.

She shrugged. "Four months. Why?"

"Has Sam ever seen a Christmas tree?"

"No," she said then winced. "Problem?"

"Not now," he said, making a final tie from the tree.

The tuxedo cat looked at Treat innocently and began to wrap around his ankles. "Oh, look," she said. "He likes you."

"No, he's trying to rub his scent on me probably because he doesn't like my human smell."

Fredericka sniffed. "I don't smell anything."

Sam gave a meow.

"Time for breakfast," she said

Treat watched as the cat proudly strode to the kitchen with its tail upright. "What are Sam's habits?"

Fredericka shrugged. "He sleeps a lot during the day. He jumps on the shelf above Leo's crib and watches over him at night. He meows if we don't respond quickly enough to Leo's cries."

"Hmm," he said as he walked around the kitchen. He glanced on the top of the refrigerator and saw several plush toys. Pulling them down, he glanced at Fredericka. "Did you put these up here?"

She glanced at the toys and frowned in confusion. "No. Two of those are Leo's toys. One is a Christmas tree ornament."

Treat nodded. "Cats are sneaky," he said.

Fredericka frowned. "Maybe so, but Sam watches over Leo, so it's okay if he takes a few toys. It's not as if Leo will notice. He has tons of toys. Christmas is coming."

"You're defending your cat against your son?"

"Sam watches over Leo. Soon enough, Leo will hold onto his toys and Sam won't get any of them." She shot him a sideways glance. "Why don't you like Sam?"

Discomfort flooded through him. "It's not Sam."

"Then what is it?"

"I brought home a kitten one time. My dad made me give it away," he confessed.

"Oh," Fredericka said, her voice full of sympathy.

"Don't feel sorry for me," he said.

"Oh, I don't," she said. "I wanted a puppy when I lived at the palace and that was a big no-go." She glanced downward. "Sam is hugging your ankles again."

Treat looked down at the cat as he wound around his feet and shook his head. "I'm telling you he doesn't like my scent, so he's trying to replace the way I smell with the way he smells."

"Is that why he's purring?" she asked, crossing her arms over her chest.

Treat heard the sound and stared at the cat. He felt a softening toward the feline. Then he shook it off. "I have no idea why he's purring."

"I do," she said. "He's purring because he likes you. He's purring because you're a guy and he's glad to have another guy in the house."

You're nuts, he wanted to say, but he didn't. "I need to get some work done. Call me if you need me." He felt the gazes of both Fredericka and Puss in Boots on him as he strode back to the guest suite. This gig was getting weird.

After making a few calls, Ericka diapered and dressed Leo for a trip to the hospital to test his hearing. Before she left, Treat stepped in front of her car and waved his hands.

"Where are you going?" he called.

She pressed down the button to push down her window. "I'm taking Leo to get his hearing checked," she said.

"Why didn't you tell me?" he asked, stepping next to her window. "It's not on the schedule you gave me."

"I didn't put all the appointments on there. The doctor told me I could wait a week or two later for testing, but I don't want to wait," she said, and shook her head. "It may sound crazy, but I need to prepare myself if he's going to have surgery. It's serious surgery," she said. "It won't be performed until after Christmas, but I don't want to wait a long time for it. This surgery could help him speak and perform just like other kids by the time he hits five or six years old. At the same time, we'll continue sign language and other therapy. It's complicated. I don't expect you to understand."

Treat shoved his hands into the pockets of his jeans. "I understand more than you think," he said.

Ericka felt a crazy connection and bit her lip. "I need to go," she said.

"Well, get into the passenger seat because I'm going with you," he said as he opened her car door.

"This is not necessary," she told him. "I can handle this on my own."

"Not this time, Princess," he said with the smile of a shark.

"Don't call me princess," she said while she rounded the car to take the passenger seat.

"Okay," he said, sliding into the driver's seat. "If I don't call you princess, what do I call you?"

"Ericka," she said through her teeth.

He drove to the hospital and she wasn't sure if she was glad for his presence or not. She squirmed in her seat and glanced back at Leo as he dozed in his infant safety seat.

"You okay?" he asked.

"I'm fine, thank you," she said.

"You don't sound fine," he said.

She took a deep breath, but didn't reply.

"What's the worst thing that could happen during this examination?" he asked.

She frowned at his question. "I hadn't thought of that."

"Well, do," he said as he drove toward the hospital. "Are you afraid he has a tumor?"

"Oh, heavens, no," she said. "No tumors. I was just hoping his hearing would improve."

"And if it doesn't?" he prompted.

"Then we'll learn sign language and he'll get surgery. The prospect of surgery terrifies me," she said, her stomach knotting.

"Will he have the surgery tomorrow?" he asked.

"No," she said, staring at him. "It will be months."

"So you'll have time to prepare," he said.

She took a deep breath. "Yes, I will."

"Take more deep breaths," he said. "You're a strong woman. You can handle this. You'll get Leo through this."

Ericka knitted her eyebrows. "How do you know that?"

"I'm an excellent judge of character," he said. "Before I met you, I thought you were a prissy princess. You've already proved you're more than that."

Nonplussed, Ericka didn't know how to respond. She wasn't sure if she should be insulted or complimented. "Why did you think I was prissy?" she asked.

"Press," he said. "Press was all wrong."

She felt a soft warmth infuse her. She sank back into her seat and smiled. "I didn't like you when I first met you."

"I know," he said.

She glanced over at him. "You're too tall, too big."

"Someone may have felt more secure because of that," he muttered.

"I found you intrusive," she said, and slit her eyes at him. "Sam didn't, though."

"Sam wants another man around the house. He likes Leo, even though he steals his toys."

"I had no idea Sam was stealing toys and ornaments," she said.

"Cats are crafty," he said.

"You like Sam," she said. "Admit it."

"I don't trust him," he said. "But he seems like a good cat."

"You don't trust easily," she said.

"I don't," he admitted.

"Neither do I," she told him and looked out the window as he pulled into the hospital parking lot.

"Want me to wait or come in?" he asked as he pulled to the outpatient entrance.

"Wait please," she said as she got out of the passenger seat. She released Leo from his infant seat and held him against her. "We'll be back in about an hour."

Treat guided the car into a parking space and sat for five minutes that felt like forever. He got out of the car and paced the parking lot for thirty minutes. He checked his watch and did a few push-ups followed by planks. Glancing at his watch, he took several breaths and paced five more times around the parking lot.

Standing next to the car, he jogged in place and looked at the door to the hospital. Finally Ericka appeared with Leo in her arms. She didn't look happy as she walked toward the car.

"Hey," he said.

"Don't ask," she said with tears in her eyes. She began to put Leo in his infant safety seat. Treat helped her. She opened the door to the passenger side of the car and stepped inside.

Treat slide inside the vehicle and started the engine. Despite the sound of the engine, the silence between Ericka and him was deafening. She must have been terribly disappointed by the test results.

He backed out of the parking space and began the drive home. After five minutes of complete silence, he spoke. "Do you know who Thomas Edison is?"

"Of course, but I don't know much about him," she said.

"He was an American inventor," he said. "He invented the light bulb and is credited as the father of electricity. He was deaf."

She took a quick sharp breath. "I didn't know that."

"Leo is going to be an amazing man. He has an amazing mother."

Ericka looked away from him, outside the window and squished her eyes together. She didn't want to cry. She really, really didn't want to cry, but tears streams out the sides of her eyes. *Oh, heaven help her.* She sniffed and prayed that Treat wouldn't hear her.

She couldn't manage a word during the rest of the trip home and she breathed a sigh of relief as Treat pulled into the driveway. "Thanks for driving us," she said.

"No problem. I'm supposed to keep you safe," he said. "Another thought. Francisco Goya was a successful deaf artist."

She met his gaze and smiled at him. "Thank you for the encouragement."

"Even bad news isn't bad news," he said. "With any kind of news, you can make a plan."

She felt the click of certainty inside her. "Thank you," she said. "Really."

He shrugged. "Anytime. Let me help you with Leo."

"I can handle it," she said.

"Of course you can," he said. "But you don't always have to."

Treat picked up the baby from his infant seat and carried him inside the front door.

"Oh, brilliant," she said, seeing a package. "It's a rotating solar toy that promises to gently light up the nursery ceiling. I ordered it a few days ago."

"It could work," he said.

"You don't believe in it," she said.

He lifted one of his hands because he was carrying Leo in the other. "It's got to be better than waving a flashlight around in the middle of the night."

She pressed her lips together. "True."

Treat took Leo to the nursery. He set the baby down in his crib. "I'll set it up for you while you change his diaper."

"Are you afraid of dirty diapers?" she asked with a sly smile.

"I wouldn't use the term *afraid*," he said, then

returned to the front door to get the package while Nanny Marley appeared in the doorway.

"Oh, you're back," she said. "I was doing a bit of laundry so I didn't hear you come in at first. Any news on little Leo's hearing?" she asked as she headed for the nursery.

"I don't think the test showed any improvement," Treat said, carrying the package.

"Oh, dear," Nanny said, and sighed. "We have so many reasons to remain positive. He is a beautiful, healthy baby."

"That, he is," Treat agreed as he allowed Nanny to precede him into the nursery.

"Why, thank you," she said. "What a lovely gentleman."

Ericka looked up at him and twitched her lips in humor. "Gentleman?"

"Hey, I know a few things about manners. I wasn't raised in a barn. Let me open this box and see what tools I'll need," he said.

"And I'll take the baby. Perhaps he could use a bit of tummy time after riding in the car," Nanny said.

"Perfect," Ericka said, lifting the baby from the crib and kissing him on both chubby cheeks. "You can do some push-ups and planks and rolling over followed by a bottle. Then you'll have the best nap ever."

Leo smiled his toothless grin in response and Ericka gave him another squeeze. Then she handed him over to Nanny.

"You're a good mother," he said, and then turned back to the project.

"Thank you," she said, then gave a soft deprecating chuckle. "I'm muddling through. Are you sure I can't help you put the solar system together?" she asked.

"I've got it," he replied. "Don't you usually have some calls to return?"

"Always," Ericka said. "I'll check in later."

Treat watched Ericka walking away, enjoying the sway of her hips. Her blond hair skimmed her shoulders and her shapely pale calves peeked beneath the dress she wore. Treat couldn't help imagining what she would look like if that dress fell from her delicate shoulders down her back, over that ripe rear end to the floor.

Then he realized he was imagining the woman he was supposed to protect naked. Treat swore under his breath and gritted his teeth. He needed to keep his distance. He needed to keep a clear head. This job would make a huge difference in his future. Treat could *not* be attracted to the princess. For too many reasons to count.

Ericka frowned as she talked to the man speaking on behalf of the country of Sergenia's royal family. "I'm sorry, but I don't understand what you're asking," she said to a man named William Monroe.

"As you know, Sergenia has two princesses and a prince to represent their kingdom, but there is so much unrest. The royal family is in danger."

"And how can I help you with that?" she asked, drumming her fingers on an end table as she pumped her crossed leg.

"The royal family of Sergenia would like to seek asylum in your country," Mr. Monroe said.

"Asylum," she echoed, automatically stiffening. She knew Stefan would never agree to such an arrangement. "Public asylum? Do you really think that's wise? If there are people who have ill will for the Sergenia family, shouldn't they be secretly sheltered?"

"Possibly, but—"

"Mr. Monroe, I know my brother will not be willing to make a public issue. If you are looking for a place for the royal family to hide, then that may be a different situation," she said.

Silence followed. "The royal family would be grateful for the opportunity to reside in your country until the unrest in Sergenia has subsided," he finally said.

Ericka bit her lip. Heaven help her, this was not her area of expertise. "I'll research the matter and get back to you."

"Please don't wait long," Mr. Monroe said, then disconnected the call.

Ericka rubbed her forehead and stood. She felt as if she'd been given a huge responsibility. If she didn't respond appropriately, then the lives of the Sergenia royal family could be at stake. She said a silent prayer as she paced the den. She knitted her hands together. She would have to convince Stefan that hiding the Sergenia royals in Chantaine was the right thing to do.

Heaven help her.

Taking a deep breath, she headed for the kitchen and fixed herself a cup of tea. Sipping it, she sank into a seat. All was quiet in the house. Surprisingly enough, Leo was still napping after his active morning and early afternoon. She half wondered if she should awaken him. She didn't want him napping so long that he wouldn't sleep tonight.

Wandering down the hall, she spotted Nanny Marley reading in the sitting room.

"He's still asleep?" Ericka asked.

Nanny looked up from her book and nodded. "Yes, ma'am. I can wake him if you like," she said.

"I hesitate to do that," she said. "Sleeping babies and all that."

"True," Nanny said. She nodded toward the video screen. "He must've worn himself out this morning."

"Maybe we should do that more often," Ericka said, then laughed.

"Perhaps," Nanny said. "We must be careful not to coddle him due to his—"

"Hearing issues," Ericka finished for the woman and nodded. "He's a strong, smart baby. He needs exercise and stimulation. Treat mentioned that he especially needs visual stimulation due to his deafness."

"That sounds right to me," Nanny said. "Although heaven knows you've exposed him to sign language. You've been as perfect a mother as could be."

Ericka sighed. "I'm not sure about that, but I'm working on it. We're so lucky to have you."

Nanny smiled. "You're a lovely girl. Leo will turn out fine. Trust my word," she said.

Ericka could only hope Nanny's words would be true. Soon enough, Leo awakened. Ericka fed him and conducted the sign language lesson even though Leo seemed a bit bored. She lifted his hands so that he could physically experience the meaning of the signs. He seemed to enjoy the physical engagement.

Deciding to take him outside for a bit, she put a tiny hat over her ears and put him into his stroller. The second she opened the gate, however, Treat appeared.

"An evening walk?" he asked, meeting her gaze.

"I thought he might enjoy it," she said. "I don't get him out often enough."

"Aside from his busy day today," he said, walking beside her.

She noticed again his height and his wide shoulders. "Do you exercise every day?"

"Five out of seven days," he said. "Why do you ask?"

"I just wondered. You seem very athletic," she said.

"I always have been," he said. "I went to college on a football scholarship. I thought my future was in football."

"But not," she said.

"An injury can change your life in an instant," he said.

"But you don't appear injured," she said.

"I exercise to compensate," he said. "I was told that another football injury could cripple me."

"Yet, you're a security man," she said. "You don't worry."

He laughed. "Security is much more mental than football. If someone tackles me, they probably won't weigh over two hundred pounds. If they do, I'll mess up my knee for a better reason than chasing pigskin."

Her respect for him went up another notch. "I'm starting to understand why Stefan chose you," she said. "Not that I like it any better."

Treat chuckled again. "I told you I would disappear into your household."

"Not yet," she said. "I didn't get a chance to look at the solar system ceiling light. What do you think?"

"Really?" he asked.

"Really," she said as she studied him.

"I want one of my own."

Ericka couldn't contain a laugh. "Why?"

"This thing is slick. Glow-in-the-dark planets with a remote control battery-operated light. I don't sleep that well, but I think this thing might lull me to sleep," he said.

"It sounds even better than I thought it would be," she said.

"If you ever decide to get rid of it..."

She smiled at him, liking his combination of toughness and masculinity. How could she explain that she liked the fact that he coveted her son's new solar system night light? How utterly strange.

Chapter Five

Despite Leo's new toy, he still didn't sleep through the night. Ericka discovered, however, that after a change and some cuddles, she could set him down in the crib and put on the solar system light and he would fall asleep. Although she was weary, her mind was busy with concerns about the Sergenian royals, not to mention the public service announcement she, a British Duke and an Italian royal would make to support clean water for everyone that was scheduled for the next day. Her sister Pippa was in town and had agreed to entertain the visitors with sightseeing and dinner after the commercial was filmed. She tossed and turned until Leo's cries awakened her early the next morning.

After feeding him, she handed him over to Nanny while she showered and got ready for the shooting of the commercial. As she fixed her hair and applied cosmetics, she realized she'd forgotten how long it took to transform herself to the polished state that was de rigueur when she lived in France with her ex-husband. Now that she was a mom, she couldn't imagine investing so much time in a daily routine.

She brushed a kiss on Leo's forehead, leaving a lipstick print. "Oops. I didn't mean to mark you," she said, and dabbed at it with her fingers.

"Oh, don't worry about it," Nanny said. "I'll take care of it. Besides, it just shows how much he's loved."

"If you say so," Ericka said skeptically. "Something tells me he won't like a lipstick print from me once he hits his teen years. Oh, heavens, I can't believe that thought crossed my mind. I'm so focused on getting him to his one-year birthday."

"And that's the way it should be," Nanny said. "I've had two teenaged children. No need to go there before necessary. I hope your photo shoot goes well."

"Thanks, Nanny," she said as she walked out the front door to where Treat stood by the car. Dressed in a jacket, white shirt and dark slacks, he looked dark and powerful. With his sunglasses hiding his eyes, he had an air of mystery.

She felt a twist of awareness at his extreme masculinity. He did nothing to tone it down, although she wasn't sure if that was even possible.

"Good morning," she said. "How are you?"

"Good," he said as he opened the passenger door then rounded the car to get inside. "And you?" He started the car and used the remote to open the gate.

"Well, thank you. You'll be happy to know the new solar system seemed to help Leo with his sleep. He woke up in the middle of the night, but then fell right back to sleep after I turned on the timed light. I wish I could say the same about my own sleep. Too much on my mind," she said. "Did you sleep well?"

"I got about four hours," he said.

She cringed. "That's not enough for me."

"I don't require much. You know how it goes. Everything gets quiet and your mind wakes up. I took a swim and that helped."

"In the middle of the night? I didn't hear you," she said, wondering what thoughts kept him awake at night.

"I hope not," he said with a chuckle.

"Maybe I should try that next time I have a hard time sleeping," she said. "Go for a swim."

"Let me know if you decide to do that," he said as he continued to drive toward the beach selected for the shooting of the public service announcement. "I don't want you drowning."

"I'll have you know I'm an excellent swimmer. I was raised on an island and my father made sure all of could swim. He didn't pay much attention to us other than that, but he was adamant that we all learn to swim well."

"He didn't pay much attention to you?" he echoed. "Don't you have several siblings? Why have children if you don't want to pay any attention to them?"

"Yes, there are six of us. He had children for the sake of progeny. Plus, if there were more of us, he could send us off to make appearances and he could go yachting. He loved his yacht. More than anything," she murmured, remembering how often he'd been absent due to his love of the sea and perhaps several women.

"Interesting," Treat said. "That wasn't in the report Stefan gave me."

"Oh, it wouldn't be. Stefan rarely says anything disparaging privately about my father and he would never put such a thing in writing. What was in that report, anyway?"

"Just every fact about you since your birth," he said.

"Oh, Lord," she said, feeling a rush of embarrassment. "I'm sure he made sure to note the face that I was the bad princess during my teenage years."

"It wasn't worded exactly that way, but…"

"I've changed," she said firmly.

"I can tell," he said. "He also gave a few details about your ex-husband."

"Stefan doesn't trust my ex-husband," she said.

"Should he?"

"I suppose not," Ericka said as she looked out the window. "I prefer not to think about him. I don't see him or have to deal with him, so to me, he doesn't exist."

"What about the fact that he is Leo's father?" he asked.

"He knew I was pregnant when I left him and he's made no effort to contact me since. Leo's birth made the news, but I've stayed out of the spotlight and I won't discuss him during interviews except to say that Leo is beautiful and growing by leaps and bounds."

"Works for me," he said, and pulled alongside the beach where several others were already setting up the commercial.

Fighting a sudden attack of nerves, she took a deep breath. "I hope this goes quickly," she muttered as he helped her out of the car.

"Why? Many women would envy your beauty," he said.

"I've never enjoyed being in front of the camera," she told him.

"But you married a filmmaker," he said.

"I wasn't in the films," she told him. "The reason I married my husband was because he took me away from Chantaine. My life wasn't studied under a microscope in France. At that time, I just wanted to escape scrutiny. The only time I had to put on a show was for a premiere or awards show."

"If you hate it so much, why did you agree to do it?"

"It's for an excellent cause. It's a very small sacrifice on my part to raise awareness. If my tiny contribution can wield influence, than I should use it." She gave a silly half smile, half moue. "Time to be a grown-up."

Treat walked behind her as she headed for the small group on the beach. She wore a simple blue dress that skimmed her curves without being too tight. Classy, feminine and, in his mind, sexy. Walking in the sand exaggerated the sway of her hips. She probably cursed the way her hair fluttered in the wind. To others, she may have appeared a smiling, friendly, blue-eyed blonde, but he knew there was a lot going on under that pale, creamy skin and "Her Highness" label.

Ericka was complicated with a heart like a mama bear for her baby and devotion to her country and sisters and brothers. She was so busy with the demands of her life that Treat wondered if she had any idea how beautiful she was. He was finding himself thinking about her far more than he should. She was a job, a means to an end. He'd protected other beautiful women. Why was she different?

He watched as she patiently did her part during

each take, and there were several. Finally, two hours later, the director appeared satisfied and Ericka took several moments to speak to each person at the shoot. She also gave Pippa a hug and thanked the Duke and Italian royal for their participation.

Treat escorted her to the car and she sank into her seat. "Thank goodness that's over," she said. "Everyone was wonderful, but we all seemed to mess up on different takes."

"Where to now?" he asked, sensing she'd felt a little trapped by the experience. It wasn't quite midday.

She glanced at him in surprise. "Home, I guess."

Treat nodded. "Home, it is."

She let out a sigh. "Well, maybe we could make one stop along the way."

Treat nodded again. "Where?"

"Gelato. There's a place in town that makes fabulous gelato, almost as good as Italian. I already know I want dark chocolate," she said. "You'll have to get some, too, but you're not allowed to choose vanilla."

Treat smiled, but mentally planned the visit in his head in order to protect Ericka from unpleasant surprises. "What if I like vanilla?"

"Then you'll have to choose that a different time," she said.

"As you wish, Your Highness," he said.

"Don't start with that now," she warned him, but laughed.

Treat hadn't seen her this playful even when she

was playing with her son. It was as if every exchange with Leo had a serious undertone. Following her directions to the gelato shop, he secured a parking spot down the block and escorted her to the shop.

"You're going to love this," she told him as he constantly watched their surroundings both inside and outside.

Two servers, one male and one female, dressed in uniforms stared at Ericka in surprise.

"Your Highness?" the young woman finally managed.

"You weren't supposed to notice," Ericka whispered and smiled. "You have the best gelato in Chantaine and I want a scoop of dark chocolate."

"Yes, of course, ma'am," the woman said as she prepared Ericka's gelato.

"What kind do you want?" Ericka asked Treat with a curious expression on her face.

"You choose," he said, his attention focused on their surroundings.

"That's no fun," she said, her face falling. "Do you prefer fruit or chocolate?"

"Fruit," he said. "I'll take the berry gelato."

Treat took a bite of his and was surprised by the vivid flavor.

"Excellent, isn't it?" she asked, savoring a bite of her own.

He watched her lick her lips and felt his gut tighten in awareness.

Suddenly the waitress came up to their table again. "Your Highness, would you possibly allow us to take a photo with you?"

Ericka wrinkled her nose. "Then everyone will think I'm playing hooky," she said.

"Oh, no," the female server said. "We can say your visit was official business."

Ericka laughed. "Okay, but I'm not sure how you can sell that. Treat, would you mind taking a photo with this lovely woman's smart phone?"

Treat nodded and took the photos. "Just give us ten minutes before you post it for the world to see," he told her. "Finish in the car?" he asked Ericka. At her nod, he escorted her to the car. He inhaled his small portion of the dessert and started the car.

"Already finished?" she asked, still taking slow bites of her own.

"I wanted to get on the road before there's a crowd," he said.

"Oh, I was so busy enjoying the outing that I forgot you're working," she said.

"Your brother wouldn't forgive me if I forgot to protect you," he said. "That's always number one."

She sighed and took her last bite of gelato. "Well, it was nice while it lasted. Hope it wasn't too much of a trial," she said, and shot him a glance from beneath her eyelashes that almost looked flirtatious.

Treat felt that pull in his gut again. He would have to put a stop to it. He'd figure out how soon enough, he promised himself. In the meantime, he shook his head. "I can't think of any man who would consider that a trial," he told her in a dry tone. At the same time, she seemed to be playing havoc with a place inside him he'd considered sewn up tight and under wraps.

"Thanks for the field trip." She sighed and leaned her head back against the headrest in the car. "Maybe my sister Bridget is right. She keeps saying I need to get out more, but I don't like leaving Leo."

"You could take him out every now and then. Has he been to the beach?"

"Not since he was an infant. I'm afraid the paparazzi will catch a photo of him wearing his hearing aids. I want to protect him as long as I can," she said.

Treat shrugged. "You could always go early in the morning and put a hat on him," he said. "For that matter, you could put him in the pool, too."

"I'll see," she said. "Like you said, my number one job is to protect him."

"Are you afraid of the questions?" he asked.

She looked away for a moment as if she didn't appreciate his query. "Perhaps. I don't have all the answers. I may never. I don't want anyone to make fun of him. That would break my heart."

"Oh, I don't know about that. You've got a strong mama-bear thing going on. If anyone caused harm to your baby in any way, I wouldn't be surprised if you broke some bones."

"That may be a slight exaggeration. I'm not normally a violent person."

"But if someone threatened Leo?"

"I like to think it would never get that far," she said.

Treat gave a short, emphatic nod and pulled the car past the gate to the front door. Cutting the engine, he rounded the car and helped her out of the vehicle.

"Thank you," she said. "My new part-time genie planned to prepare an afternoon meal today. Would you like to join us?"

"Thanks," he said, knowing such a move would be dangerous. "But I have computer work."

Her eyes darkened with a twinge of disappointment. "Of course. Ciao, then," she said as she walked into the cottage.

Treat stood there, looking after her, for a full moment after she closed the door behind her. His attraction to her was ridiculous. She was the princess of a Mediterranean island for Pete's sake. He was a wrong-side-of-the-tracks kid from Texas. He knew he wasn't the kind of man who would normally catch her eye. He had to be careful. He knew enough about security to know that these situations could be emotionally intense for some people although he'd never had a problem before. He sure as shooting didn't need a problem now, especially since this job could help him expand his company internationally. He'd worked hard the past several years. He didn't want to lose all his hard-won progress just because he was developing a stupid crush on a princess.

Raking his hand through his hair, he returned to the guest suite and turned on his laptop then grabbed one of the jars of peanut butter he'd brought with him from the States and slapped a peanut butter sandwich together before he returned to his desk. The welcome screen rose to greet him. There was always work to do, he told himself. Work that would help him forget everything he had lost so quickly in his college year. Work was a panacea. Always.

Treat checked the perimeter several times then knocked on the door to the house that evening. Nanny answered. "How are you tonight, Mr. Walker?"

"I'm fine. How are you, the princess and the baby?" he asked.

"All well. The baby appears quite charmed with his new ceiling mobile of the solar system. Her Highness has either been working all afternoon or playing sign language games with Leo. I swear that woman hardly ever stops. I would just like to see her get a full night's rest."

Treat smiled and nodded. He could always count on Nanny giving him a mouthful of information. "I'm glad to hear everything is going well. I hope everyone has a good evening. I'm only a few steps away. Call me if you need me."

"Yes, sir," she said.

Treat returned to his suite and made a few calls.

His agreement with Stefan allowed him to continue to make future business plans and contacts. So far, it was quiet job, but he never let down his guard. Not even when he slept. He'd set multiple alarms and had a backup with the palace.

Hours later, he looked at the clock and realized he needed to hit the sack. He did a weight work-out in the suite, but still felt restless, so he put on a swimsuit and went to the pool. Lap after lap, he took then felt a slight disturbance in the water. Rising, he looked around and saw Ericka hanging on to the side of the wall.

He took several breaths. "What are you doing here?" he asked.

"You said you swim when you can't sleep. Why can't I do the same?" she asked.

He studied her for a long, hard moment and saw that she wasn't being coquettish. She, like him, just wanted a decent night of sleep. "Have you tried meditation?" he asked.

She sighed. "The trouble with meditation is that I keep interrupting the oms with what I worry about."

He chuckled, easily identifying with her quandary, although he struggled with more regrets than worries. "Okay, start your laps. I'll sit on the side to make sure you're okay."

"I'll do fine," she told him with a prim frown and began swimming.

He couldn't fault her form and he liked that she

didn't move too quickly. A nice, steady pace. She did a flip turn against the wall and he was impressed yet again. On her back, she kicked like a pro. After the next turn, she did a great breaststroke, tagged the wall and did another length of breaststroke.

She smiled as she approached him, taking several heaving breaths. "I was never good at butterfly."

"Looks like you're good at everything else," he said.

She gulped in several more breaths. "Again, my father encouraged competitive swimming."

"That can be good and bad," he said.

"It was probably one of the few good things he did," she said. "I need a few more laps."

She did a few more and he couldn't help admiring her body. He liked her combination of athleticism and feminine softness. She relied on the breaststroke for a couple more laps then turned on her back and did the backstroke for two more laps.

She grabbed the side of the pool and gasped for breath. "I think that's enough for now," she said.

"Should you have stopped sooner?" he asked.

"No. You always have to push yourself when you're swimming," she said, still taking deep breaths. "Even if you feel like you're dying."

"And this is why I want you to let me know if you decide to do night swimming," he said.

"Spoilsport," she said as she rested her head on

the side of the pool. "The water feels nice at night, doesn't it?"

He nodded. "Do you worry about Leo at night?"

"Yes," she said. "I worry about what I may have done during my pregnancy that caused his deafness."

"Isn't this a genetic issue?"

"Most likely," she said. "But I still wonder. I wonder if I could have prevented it."

"You couldn't have," he said.

"How can you be so confident? How can you know that I did everything possible to protect Leo during my pregnancy?"

"Because I know you did. I know you couldn't prevent his deafness," he said. "And you can't make his world perfect now. It's okay that you can't. You just need to be his mom and love him no matter what. You can't fix everything. You don't have to."

Ericka sighed. "I wish I had superpowers and could fix everything."

"Stop wishing," he said. "Just do what you can every day. You get to the end of the day, say a prayer and enjoy a full night of rest every night."

She chuckled. "A full night of rest every night?" she echoed. "That's a fantasy world for me."

"Do another four laps," he said.

"I'm tired," she protested.

"Not tired enough," he told her. "You're still arguing."

She groaned, but did the laps, albeit slowly. After

the fourth, she dragged herself out of the pool. "You're not as bad as my father, but you're close. I'm way tired."

"Good. Maybe you'll sleep now," he said. "Let Nanny do her job if Leo awakens during the night."

"It makes me feel like a slacker when I don't get up with him at night," she said.

"Take a break. It's not as if you have a husband to take a turn," he said.

Ericka bit her lip. "And that's another subject. No father figure for him."

"He's got plenty of father figures. More than most," Treat said. "Your brothers. Your brothers-in-law. I hear there's more one road to Mecca. You're taking it."

"If you say so," she said, wrapping a towel around her.

"I do. Now you're growing very sleepy. Very sleepy. Your eyes are closing," he said.

"You're a good guy, Treat, but you're no hypnotist."

"Bet you fall asleep within five minutes," he said.

"But will I stay asleep?" she asked.

"Yes," he said, then waited until she left to swim ten more laps. He wanted Ericka more than ever.

Chapter Six

The next night, Ericka sent Treat a text informing him that she planned to take Leo for an early morning trip to the ocean. Ericka had strange feelings about Treat. He showed her a lot of heart then totally backed away as if he wanted to remain as professional as possible.

That's what he should do, she told herself as she crawled into bed and pulled the sheets up to her chin. That's what she and Stefan wanted. A true professional. It was his good heart that was wearing her down. It was his good heart that made her feel both weak and strong. And she totally needed to get over those feelings.

She took a deep breath and tried the meditation

exercise she'd learned earlier in the day, and surprisingly enough, she drifted off to sleep.

Reality smudged with dreams. *Treat took her into his arms and his body felt so strong and muscular. His heartbeat drummed against her chest.*

"I want you," he confessed. "I want you, but I shouldn't."

She felt herself melt in his arms. "I want you, too. I was afraid I was the only one."

"No," he said, and lowered his mouth to hers. He slid his tongue between her lips and she drank in the taste of him. She couldn't prevent herself from rubbing her chest against his.

He groaned in response. "You feel so good," he said. "I want more of you," he told her. "I want you naked."

Her heart beat so quickly she wondered if she would faint. She slid her fingers through his short hair and opened her mouth for a soulful kiss.

Moments later, as if through magic, her clothes floated away, as did his. Her nipples meshed against his hard chest. She felt him naked against her from head to toe. He took her mouth and the kiss seemed to go on forever and ever.

"I can't get enough of you," he muttered against her lips as he slid his hand between them and rubbed her where she was swollen and needy. "Can't get enough."

"I want you," she said. "I need you..."

Groaning, he pushed her legs apart and...

Ericka reached for him, arching her body. "Treat..."

A sound permeated her dream. A baby crying. Ericka sat up in bed, fully aroused and full of want and need. She gasped for breath and shook her head, chasing consciousness. "Oh, my—"

She shook her head again and realized she was hearing Leo's cry. Rubbing her forehead, she climbed from her bed and went to the nursery. She clicked on the light for the solar system and waited a few seconds. She could hear Leo squirming in his crib then he quieted. She felt him slurp his thumb into his mouth as he studied the lights on the ceiling.

He was comforting himself, she realized. He needed a little extra help, but he was working at it, sucking his thumb and staring at the solar system. Her chest tightened and she felt a tear run down her cheek at the realization. Her baby boy was doing the best he could. She would do the best she could for him even if the best she could do frightened her nearly to death.

Ericka returned to bed and waited for sounds from Leo, but he remained quiet, hopefully sleeping. She tried meditation, but she fell asleep during the middle of it. Proof she was exhausted, but also felt safe. She would have to think about that safe feeling tomorrow. Or the next day.

* * *

The next morning, Ericka arose to the sound of her alarm and dragged herself out of bed. Despite her drowsiness, excitement raced through her. She was taking Leo to the beach!

She stripped then pulled on her bathing suit followed by a pair of shorts and a t-shirt. She went to her bathroom, splashed her face with water and brushed her teeth.

"Your Highness?" Nanny said, wearing her night robe, as Ericka entered the hallway. "I believe the baby is asleep."

"For how long?" Ericka asked.

"Most of the night," the older woman said. "I only heard him once and he quickly went back to sleep or I would have gotten up with him."

"It's the solar system," Ericka whispered. "I pray it continues to work. In the meantime, I'm taking him to the beach."

Nanny's eyes widened. "The beach? Are you sure that's wise? Won't the water be too cool for him?"

"If it is, he can enjoy the sand. This baby lives on an island and he's only been to the beach once. I want him to experience the ocean, if only for a few minutes."

Nanny gave a thoughtful nod. "I think it's a good idea. The boy loves new experiences."

Ericka smiled, glad Nanny approved of her idea. Even though Ericka knew it was the right thing to do,

Nanny's affirmation added to her confidence. "See you later," she said. "Go back to bed."

"As you wish, ma'am," Nanny said, tightening the belt of her robe and returning to her room.

Ericka rushed to the nursery and broke one of her cardinal rules. She awakened Leo. He blinked his sleepy eyes and rubbed them then met her gaze as she changed his diaper.

"Good morning," she whispered, even though she knew he couldn't hear him. She signed the words and repeated them then smiled.

He smiled his toothless grin in return.

"Aren't you handsome," she said to him and stroked his forehead. She grabbed a few more articles of clothing and a bottle. He was hungry and quickly downed the formula. Ericka lifted him against her shoulder and a burp escaped. "Aren't you the efficient one this morning?" she asked, then grabbed her diaper bag and raced out the door.

Treat was waiting next to the car. Her heart leaped at the sight of him. She told herself to ignore her wayward reaction to him.

"You think he's ready for the ocean?" he asked.

"We'll start with the sand and end with the ocean. I don't want him to get too cold," she said, and placed Leo in the infant safety seat. "I think he's ready for an adventure."

"He's always ready for an adventure," Treat said.

She glanced at him. "And how do you know that?"

Treat shrugged. "He's just that kind of guy."

Ericka stuck a pacifier in Leo's mouth and he suckled it for all he was worth, as if he knew this would be one of his first great adventures.

Sliding into the passenger seat, Ericka gave Treat direction to the privately owned beach of the Devereaux family. Although the beach was private, it was no match for the long lenses of cameras from the paparazzi. Since it was December and early morning, however, they had a great shot at avoiding the photographers.

Treat pulled down a sandy road and stopped when the beach was in sight. "I think we're here."

"I think we are," she said, excitement thrumming through her. Pulling on a baseball cap, she got out of the car before Treat could assist her and started to release Leo from his safety seat. She began to pick him up.

"Hat," Treat reminded her, and she paused.

"Right. Thanks," she said as she put a ball cap on the baby's head.

Leo stared at her, still sucking on his pacifier. His expression seemed to say, *Are you sure you know what you're doing? I don't know if I like this thing on my head.*

"You're gonna love the cap," she told him and pulled him against herself.

The trio walked toward the gentle lap of the waves on the beach. Not too far from the surf, she sank onto the sand and put Leo between her legs. "How do you like this?" she asked, and stroked his head while keeping his cap in face.

Leo continued to suck on his pacifier as he stared at the surf.

Ericka lifted a handful of sand and spilled it over his tiny palm. He glanced down at his hand and she repeated the motion. His sucking slowed as he studied the sand in his hand. A few seconds later, he dipped his hand into the sand and squeezed his fingers through it.

"Good for you," she said, patting his arm. "You're a smart one."

Leo played in the sand for the next several moments and Ericka loved watching him explore.

"Are you sure you want to try the ocean? It may be a bit cold," Treat said.

"I agree," she said. "Maybe we could just dip his feet in it."

Treat grabbed Leo against him and pulled Ericka rise to her feet. They took a few steps into the ocean.

"A little chilly," she said.

"We can let him have his own opinion," Treat said and, still holding Leo against him, he dipped the baby's feet in the ocean.

Leo paused again in suckling his pacifier.

"How was that for you, big guy?" he asked, and then dipped his tiny feet into the surf again.

Leo kicked his feet and legs.

Ericka laughed. "I don't know if that's a yes or no."

"He's not screaming, so let's call it a yes," Treat said as he dipped the baby's feet in a wave once more. Leo opened his mouth and cackled, dropping his pacifier. Treat caught the paci before it fell into the ocean.

Ericka stretched out her hands for Leo, and Treat passed the baby to her. "You may be an ocean baby, after all," she said. "We'll have to bring you again."

"Are you going to take a dip?" Treat asked.

"Not this time," she said. "It's a little cool for me."

He nodded, staring out at the ocean. "I only went to the ocean twice when I was growing up. Loved it both times. Once, we went in winter and I swam even though it was freezing cold," he said, then chuckled.

"You should go now," she urged.

He shook his head. "I can't be protecting you if I'm swimming in the ocean."

She sighed. "Well, darn."

"I'll come back another time on my day off," he said.

"What day off?" she asked as they walked out of the water. "You haven't taken a day off since you started."

"I will sometime," he said.

"But then I won't get to see you swim in the ocean," she said.

"I'm sure I wouldn't win any prizes for form," he told her. "You won't be missing much."

"I bet you dive into the waves," she said.

He looked at her and his lips lifted in a half-grin. "Who are you? The psychic princess?"

She walked on the sand toward the car. "That's what I want to see. You diving into the waves."

"Why?" he asked.

"I'd like to see what you were like as a kid," she said.

He shook his head. "The kid in me doesn't come out very often. The kid had a complicated childhood."

"How complicated?"

"I told you more than enough. You're a client," he reminded her.

His statement felt like a smack in her face. She took a quick breath. "You were just part of an amazing, private experience. How many times have you taken a baby with his mom for a dip in the ocean?"

"Never," he admitted.

"Leo and I are not just clients," she told him tersely, and put Leo into his car seat. "Do you have his pacifier?"

"Here," he said, and pressed the pacifier into her hand.

He opened the passenger door and she slid into her seat without looking at him. She heard and felt Treat get into the car and start the ignition. She kept her gaze trained forward. She was so incredibly insulted and not sure why. Why should she care what staff thought of her?

"Sorry," he said as he pulled past the gate to the front door and stopped. "That was out of line. I've dealt with kids before, but not infants. And not you. I just need to keep my head on straight."

Her heart turned over at the intent expression on his face. His gaze forced her to think more about how she was feeling at this moment. This *was* a job for him, one that would end. He was a human being with feelings. Deeper feelings than she'd expected. He was the first man who'd inspired crazy emotions inside her. Emotions she hadn't felt in a long time. The situation was very complicated, but that didn't change the fact that she wanted him.

"I understand," she said. "I'll get Leo inside for his bottle and a nap."

"And your morning full of work," he said, stepping out of the car. He unhooked Leo from his car seat. "You did good, big guy," he murmured to the baby. "Want me to bring him inside?"

"I can do it," she said, taking Leo into her arms. She inhaled his baby scent and gave him a kiss on his chubby cheek. "Thank you," she said, and walked into the cottage. Feeling Treat's gaze on her as she walked, Ericka felt a tiny sliver of comfort. He was as affected by her as she was by him. She wasn't completely alone. Small comfort, she told herself. Neither could do anything about their feelings.

Ericka looked down at Leo as he stared up at

her. Maybe doing nothing was for the best. She had enough on her hands and in her arms.

That afternoon Ericka decided to pay a visit to the palace. She needed to talk to Stefan personally. Despite the fact that her biggest concern was Leo, thoughts of the Sergenian royals plagued her. She needed to get Stefan on her side.

Treat insisted on driving her and she did all she could not to think about the dream she'd had the other night and how much he affected her and how hard it was to be this close to him. When they arrived at the palace, she nearly leaped out of the car. "I'll be back soon."

She'd called ahead and Stefan had agreed to meet with her provided she wasn't complaining about security. Truth was, her security could complain about her, but that was another story.

His assistant opened his office door at her second knock. "Your Highness," the assistant said.

"Good afternoon," she said as she walked toward Stefan.

He stepped from behind his desk and kissed her on the cheek. "You sounded upset," he said.

She kissed him on the cheek in return. "I'm concerned. I received a call about the royal family of Sergenia."

"The country has experienced a lot of unrest," he said.

She nodded. "The royal family is in danger. They need a place to go."

He gave her a thoughtful look. "You know we don't get involved in the politics of other countries."

"This isn't about politics," she said. "It's about people. What if one of us had needed a place to go because Chantaine had become more violent?"

"We take care of our people," he said. "We put our people first. That's why Chantaine is peaceful."

"But this isn't asking a lot. They just need a place to disappear," she said.

Stefan shook his head. "I appreciate your good heart, but I have to think about the greater good. I don't want violent people from Sergenia taking revenge on our citizens."

"But if we kept it secret—"

"Fredericka," he said. "The answer is no."

She understood her brother's point, but her heart still tugged at the thought of the young Sergenian royals in danger. She'd done research on them. They were good people.

She bit her lip. "You know I could have done this behind your back."

He narrowed his eyes in a way that would have intimidated her five years ago. Not so much today. "I hope your honor as a Devereaux means more to you than that."

"I hope you'll think about the Devereaux honor and how we're trying to make a new name for ourselves. Please reconsider." She lifted her hand when he opened his mouth. "Don't say anything, just please reconsider. Have a good evening in your very safe palace, in your very safe country. Not all are quite so fortunate," she said as she walked out of his office.

Striding out of the palace, she found Treat waiting for her just outside the door. He quickly exited the car and assisted her inside. Ericka jerked her seatbelt into place.

"That was fast," he said, sliding back into his seat and pulling out of the parking area.

"Fast, but not successful. Being honest and honorable can be a total pain," she muttered.

Ericka felt Treat's gaze on her as he stopped at a stop sign. "Honor? Honest? You want to explain?"

"Not really," she said, feeling extremely frustrated. "Everyone thinks I have this superficial job where all I do is plan meetings with other members of royalty, but other things can happen. I can get calls that are more than fluff. What am I supposed to do about those calls?"

"What are you talking about?" he asked.

Ericka took a deep breath and crossed her arms over her chest. "Nothing."

"Doesn't sound like nothing to me, but as long as it doesn't affect your security," he said.

"Of course it doesn't affect my security," she said, and sighed. "It affects the security of the royals in Sergenia, but if you repeat that, I truly will kill you."

He gave a whistle. "Sergenia. Oh, that place is a mess."

"Yes, it is, and the royals need a place to go," she said.

"Here? Chantaine? Why here?" he asked. "Why not a larger country?"

"You must agree we're a bit more isolated. We're not a target," she said.

"True, I guess. I take it Stefan didn't agree."

"He didn't, but I'm not giving up," she said. "I put in the initial guilt screws. I'll try again in a few days."

He glanced at her and chuckled. "You're a little scary when you get determined."

She smiled back at him. "I'll take that as a compliment."

Shortly later, they arrived back at the cottage and Ericka thanked Treat as she entered the house. Nanny greeted her, holding Leo in her arms.

"He's been a bit fussy this afternoon. The hearing doctor called the house phone. I couldn't get to it in time. I think he left a message."

Ericka glanced at her cell phone and spotted a missed call from Leo's doctor. She listened to the message and her stomach fell. The doctor confirmed what she had already sensed. Leo was profoundly deaf. But he could have life changing surgery in January or February.

The news left her in a quandary because the surgery presented a fair amount of risk. The possibility of endangering Leo crippled her. In normal circumstances, she would want to put it off. The flip side was that if Leo's surgery was successful, he would be able to speak normally and hear more than he ever could with hearing aids.

Ericka went to Nanny and extended her arms. "I'd like to hold him for a while," she said.

"Of course," Nanny said. "Simon left groceries and dinner. Would you like some soup?"

"That sounds perfect," Ericka said as she carried Leo to the den. He stared up at her with his wide blue eyes. "How are you doing, little man? I thought you would be all tuckered out from your adventure in the ocean this morning."

Leo squirmed in her arms and Ericka realized her darling baby had gas. "Maybe I can help," she said, sitting down and putting his tummy over her knees. He gave several burps and let air out his backside then seemed to relax.

She pulled him onto her lap. "Better now?"

He made a moue, but didn't cry. "Bet you're hungry now," she said. "Let's get a bottle." She went to the kitchen and pulled a bottle from the refrigerator as Nanny heated soup on the stove.

"Gas," Ericka said.

"That explains the crankiness. I hope he'll sleep well tonight," Nanny said.

"Me, too," Ericka said as she gave Leo his bottle.

He sucked it down in no time. She burped him repeatedly then put him to bed. He was so drowsy he looked as if he were craving rest.

Crossing her fingers, Ericka returned to the kitchen and accepted the bowl of soup Nanny had heated for her. "Thank you so much," she said. "It's been quite a day."

"I'll say," Nanny said. "You've been up since nearly the crack of dawn. I bet you're ready for some sleep yourself."

"I am, but I hate for you to take the tortured night shift," Ericka said as she sipped her soup.

"Remember, I can sleep when he does. You have work to do. Don't you worry about me," Nanny replied, and patted Ericka's back.

But Ericka couldn't help feeling *she* should be the one getting up with Leo.

Chapter Seven

Despite her qualms, Ericka gave into her longing for a full night's rest and allowed Nanny to take the night shift. She heard a couple of peeps from the baby monitor, but no prolonged crying. When she rose, she felt rested and refreshed, a condition she rarely experienced these days.

Making her way into the kitchen, she found Nanny sneezing into a tissue. "Bless you and good morning," Ericka said. "I hope Leo didn't keep you up too much last night."

"Not at all, ma'am, but I fear I'm getting a cold. I've been washing my hands, but I feel as if I need to spray myself with anti-germ cleaner so I won't pass this on to you or the baby," Nanny said then sneezed again.

"You look miserable," Ericka said. "Perhaps you should take a day or two to recuperate."

"I hate to leave you without help," Nanny said.

"I have Simon for food and errands. You've just given me the gift of a full night of sleep. I think I can manage for a couple days."

"Are you sure?"

Ericka nodded. "You'll get better sooner if you rest. And take some of Simon's soup with you. He made quite a bit of it," she said, going to the refrigerator and pulling out the crock of soup. She poured some into a storage container and gave it to Nanny.

"You're too good to me," Nanny said.

"Not at all," Ericka said. "I hope you feel better soon."

Nanny left for her small apartment in town and Ericka quickly took a shower then started working on a spreadsheet of workshops for the upcoming conference. In the middle of a telephone call with one of the prospective speakers, she heard Leo cry out. Quickly ending the call, she went to the nursery, changed his diaper and brought him into the den with her. She gave him his bottle, made the sign for milk and moved his hand to make the same sign.

Leo clapped his hand against hers and cackled.

Ericka couldn't resist smiling. "We'll keep working on it," she said, while he sucked down his formula. As soon as he finished, she burped him several times. A gassy baby was not a happy baby.

"Time for sign language class," she said, then clicked on the pre-recorded video on her laptop. Sitting on the floor, she propped Leo on her lap and repeated the words from the tutor and performed the signs then helped move his hands into the signs.

A knock sounded at the front door and she glanced toward it. Who—

Treat poked his head inside and she felt an unwelcome surge of pleasure at just the sight of him. *Oh, please. Get a grip*, she told herself.

"Just checking on you. I noticed Nanny left earlier."

"We're fine. Nanny was fighting a cold and losing, so I thought it would be best for everyone for her to take a couple days off."

"Good call," he said. "How's he doing with sign language?"

She chuckled and shook her head. "I think he's more interested in giving me a high five and having fun, but I've been told most babies don't start signing until six months."

"Nothing wrong with both of you having fun," he said. "He's a fun kid."

She felt a slight easing inside her and let out a breath. "I'm trying so hard to do everything correctly that I sometimes forget about having fun."

"Think about when you were a kid. Didn't you learn better when you were having fun?" he asked.

She thought back to her childhood and remembered strict nannies and teachers. There had been one or two that had relaxed the rules at times. "I guess you're right."

Sam strolled into the room and began to rub his face on Treat's jeans. He looked down at the cat in confusion. "He does this nearly every time I come into the house. Doesn't he know that I'm not really a cat person?"

Amused, she tried to keep a serious face. "It's obvious that he's determined to make you love him," she said.

Treat rolled his eyes, but bent down to rub the cat behind his ears. Sam closed his eyes in contentment.

Leo squirmed and let out a little shriek, waving his hands toward Sam. Hearing the baby, Sam obligingly strolled next to Ericka and Leo. Leo patted the cat. He hadn't quite learned the technique of stroking. Sam tolerated the petting then slinked toward the kitchen.

"Does the cat always let Leo pet him?" Treat asked.

"More times than not," she said, rising from the floor. "I think Sam believes his job is to watch Leo."

"A watch cat instead of a watch dog," he said. "Looks like it's working. I'll let you get back to whatever you're doing."

"I'm getting ready to eat lunch. Simon brought soup and a pasta meal that could feed a dozen. Would you like to join us?" she asked.

She saw a flicker of hesitation, as if he wanted to stay. He shook his head and she hated the knot of disappointment she felt in the pit of her stomach.

"Thanks, but I'll have to pass," he said.

Why? she wanted to ask, but swallowed the question. She wasn't asking for a lifetime commitment. She just wanted a little company, and the more time she spent with him, the more curious she became about him. But he was clearly determined to keep his distance. She should accept that and be done with her thoughts about him.

Deliberately forcing herself to stop thinking about Treat, she made sure Leo got in some tummy time, watching him grunt and groan as he did baby push-ups. She placed one of his favorite toys in his peripheral vision to see if she could tempt him to roll over. He worked hard but wasn't quite ready. When he started to cry, she scooped him and gave him the toy, praising him even though she knew he couldn't hear him. She wanted to stay in the habit of praising him for the day when he could hear her, possibly after his surgery in January.

He was drooling like a fountain and rubbing his eyes, so she put him down for his afternoon nap and returned to her work. Less than an hour later, she heard him crying. Surprised, she turned on his solar system toy. That only worked for a few more minutes. She brought him with her into the den and put him in his infant seat with toys hanging in front of him, but he continued to fuss.

She spent most of the rest of the afternoon walking the floor with him in his arms. Fearing he might be catching Nanny's cold, she touched his face and body, but he didn't appear to have a fever. He did, however, seem to be chewing on his pacifier more than sucking on it.

"You're teething," she said, feeling like a dumb bunny. "Maybe some ice?"

The night turned into an endless search of relief for Leo's sore gums. She felt as if she tried everything, but nothing worked for more than fifteen minutes.

Changing into her pajamas, Ericka rocked Leo in the rocking chair beside his bed. He calmed and she put him in his crib then headed for her own bed. Not long later, he cried again and Ericka tried the solar system, but it was clear that Leo was hurting. She rocked him again, put him down and headed again for her bed. Just as she fell asleep, Leo cried out again.

For the five hundredth time during the past four months, Ericka encountered the truth again: *this is single motherhood*. Sometimes it was one day at a time. Other times it was five minutes at a time. Tonight was the latter. She rocked then turned on the solar system light until it all became a blur. Sometime after midnight, she wondered if this night would ever end.

Treat took a swim and looked at the lights in the cottage. He noticed that some form of light kept illuminating the nursery. The room went dark and he swam a few more laps then paused. The light from the nursery flickered on again.

Deciding to give it a few more minutes, he returned to the guest suite, took a shower and pulled on sweat pants and a tank. Restless, he walked outside and looked at the nursery window. The light was on. Well, darn. He was going to have to do something.

Treat waited a few more moments and the room went dark. Edgy, he decided to check on the princess and her baby. He unlocked the door, approving of the fact that Ericka had indeed locked it, and walked down the hall to the nursery. The door was ajar, so he walked inside to silence. Ericka was crumpled into a rocking chair, clearly asleep. Treat walked closer to the crib and saw that Leo was sprawled on his back, also asleep.

Putting his hands on his hips, Treat assessed the situation. He definitely didn't want to wake the baby, but Ericka needed to be in bed. As soon as possible. Taking a silent deep breath, he approached her and touched her arm. She didn't awaken. It must have been a rough evening, he thought. Sliding his hands underneath her, he picked her up and carried her to her room.

He gently put her on her bed and her eyelids flickered. She looked up at him and batted her eyes again, as if to clear them. "Treat?"

"Yeah," he said, his face inches from her.

Her eyebrow wrinkled. "What—"

"You fell asleep in the nursery and looked uncomfortable, so I brought you back to your bed," he said.

"Leo?" she asked and his heart softened because she automatically asked about her son even though she wasn't totally conscious.

"He's sleeping. Looks like a deep sleep," he said.

"Oh, thank goodness. Poor thing. He's teething," she said.

"Ah," he said, unable to pull away from her.

For a fraction of a second, she lowered her eyelids then looked him straight in the eye. "Thank you," she whispered and wrapped her hand around his neck and kissed him.

Her mouth was so soft and sweet he immediately wanted more. He wanted to taste her. And heaven forbid, take her. He slid his tongue past her lips and tasted a delicious combination of citrus and mint. He felt her lift her fingers through his hair and a rush of arousal raced through him.

Her combination of sweet and spicy undid him. Treat couldn't stop himself from devouring her mouth. She opened easily to him, making him want more and more. She pulled him down against her. He gave into her urging and relished the sensation of her warm, feminine body beneath his. It would be all too easy to kiss away her nightclothes then kiss her all over her body. All too easy to touch her in all her secret places and make her ready and wanting for him. All too easy to thrust inside...

Treat was suddenly so hard with need he trembled from it. She kissed him again, thrusting her sweet tongue in his mouth. He swallowed a thousand curses at how she made him feel. Strong, tender, fierce. Out of control.

He couldn't get out of control. He could not.

Even as she wriggled beneath him and took him with her mouth, he knew he needed to draw back. For her sake and his.

It was tough, but he did it. He pulled back, gasping for air. "Whoa," he muttered.

"Wow," she said, her eyelids half-shuttering her eyes in a sexy glance. She slid her hands down his shoulders to his arms.

She made him feel strong, sexy and all too aware of the fact that he hadn't been with a woman in a long time. But she was different. She wasn't just any woman.

"I didn't mean for that to happen," he said.

"But it was a good thing to happen," she said. The expression in her eyes was so inviting he had to look away.

"Can't deny that," he admitted, and kissed her on her cheek. Her lips were far too dangerous. "You need sleep," he said. "Get it while you can."

"I won't forget that kiss," she whispered.

"Neither will I," he said, and forced himself to rise from the bed. Then he forced himself to walk out of her bedroom and out of the cottage. His body was hot, his heart was hammering in his chest and he was hard with want and need. Returning to the guest suite, he headed straight for the bathroom. He stripped off his clothes and stepped into a cold shower. Standing under the cold spray, he waited for relief from his need for Ericka. He waited for fifteen minutes, but relief never arrived.

Leaving the shower, he dried himself off and pulled on a pair of underwear. He went to his self-made gym and began to work out. An hour later, his muscles were tired, but his brain still drifted toward the sensation of Ericka's body and mouth beneath his. He wondered if he would ever be able to rid himself of the memory.

Ericka slept like the dead until Leo's cry awakened her from the baby monitor. Stumbling from her bed, she walked to the bedroom and spotted Sam mewing on the shelf above Leo. "Okay, okay," she said. "I'm here."

She looked down at Leo and put her hand on his tummy. "How are you feeling today, sweetie?"

Leo squirmed and wiggled then smiled at her. Ericka's heart squeezed tight. "Good for you, sweetheart," she cooed as she changed his diaper. "How are your gums? Are they a little better?" she asked.

Leo giggled and her heart caught again.

"You are clearly a morning guy," she said while she lifted him into her arms. Carrying him to the kitchen, she pulled a bottle from the fridge and sat in the den and fed him. Burping was compulsory and she squeezed several gas bubbles from him.

"So let's do little sign language while you're fresh," she said, turning on a video lesson.

She lifted his hands to follow the signs during the lessons, but again, Leo seemed to prefer playing patty-cake. She laughed. "Come on. Give me a try for cat. You can do that," she said, pointing at Sam who stared at them as if they crazy. She gave the sign of stroking a cat's whiskers and helped Leo do the same. "Cat," she repeated.

Sensing he was being discussed, Sam came closer and allowed Leo to pet him. He gave a meow then walked away. Leo grunted and waved toward Sam.

"Leo loves Sam, doesn't he?" she said then gave her baby a squeeze.

Leo wasn't drooling quite as much today, so she hoped he would rest more comfortably during his naps. She put him down for his morning nap and was surprised that he slept soundly, but Ericka was no fool. She used the time to make several phone calls and get work done. When he awakened over an hour later, Ericka fed him and kept him awake until he grew cranky. Then she put him to bed.

After that, Ericka couldn't stop thinking about Treat and how his body had felt against hers, how his mouth had felt against hers. She couldn't remember when she had felt more like a woman, more wanted in a man's arms. She could still taste him on her lips.

Her heart hammered in her chest at the thought of him. She wanted to be with him, to feel his mouth on hers, to feel him on her…inside her.

Ericka bit her lip, thinking and plotting and planning. The last time she'd attempted to seduce a man, it had been her ex-husband. This, her second time, she planned to seduce her bodyguard and the thought of it made her so nervous she could hardly stand it.

Leo was cooperative. He awakened early evening and she fed and played with him. Apparently his gums weren't hurting tonight. Great for her and him.

She rocked him to sleep and he easily settled into sleep. It seemed like a miracle to her. Or, perhaps, destiny, she thought, and dressed in a skimpy black tank dress. She fluffed her hair and said a crazy prayer then pressed the intercom button for Treat. "Do you mind coming over to the cottage?"

"No problem. I'll be right over," Treat said.

Ericka sat on the sofa. Then she stood. Then she sat down again.

Treat walked through the front door. "Problem?" he asked.

"Yes," she said, her heart thumping in her chest. "My problem is that I want you very, very much."

Treat took a deep breath. "Ericka," he said.

"I've put my feelings on a plate. Can you do the same?" she asked.

Treat closed his eyes and looked away. "You know this is wrong," he finally said.

"Wrong?" she echoed, rising from the sofa. "But we're adults. We can determine what's best for us."

Treat shook his head. "I can't do this," he said. "If I'm with you, I don't know how I can be rational and protect you the way I need to," he said. "It's not that I don't want you," he said.

Ericka struggled with his rejection. "Right," she said, trying to figure out her next step since her first step had clearly failed.

"No, really—"

"Oh, stop," she said. "You clearly have no problem resisting my attempt at seduction. Enough humiliation. Let's just go to our separate beds."

"You're wrong," he said, moving toward her. "I do want—"

"Stop," she said, lifting her hand. "I made a mistake and now we're both uncomfortable. Let's just try to forget it all."

"I can't do that," he said.

"You may have an easier time than I will," she

said. "Good night, or as my sister-in-law Eve would say, sweet dreams."

Ericka walked to her bedroom and stripped off her dress. She suddenly felt a century old and as sexy as a stone. Humiliated, she put on her comfy jammies and climbed into her bed. Treat was not in her future and she needed to forget that mind-blowing kiss they'd shared. It had been an illusion. He might say that he wanted her, but he clearly didn't want her as much as she wanted him.

She needed to shut those desires and needs down. Now and forever.

The following afternoon, Nanny returned appearing less congested and more rested.

Ericka decided she needed a little outing, so she told Treat she wanted to visit her sister but also told him she wanted to drive herself. He could follow in his own vehicle. After her failed attempt at seduction last night, she couldn't bear the prospect of him in such close quarters with her.

Driving her small car onto Bridget's ranch, she pulled to a stop and skipped to the front door. She knocked.

Seconds later, Bridget, immensely pregnant, opened the door and squealed. "You're here. Where's the baby?"

"Resting," Ericka said. "I just needed a sister visit."

"Well, you've got one. Come on inside," Bridget said, and led her inside to a comfortable sunroom. "You picked a good day. The twins are in a quiet mood. Playing Lego. Under all that quietness, I'm convinced they're trying to take over the world. My husband says swelling from my pregnancy is making me crazy, but I know better."

Ericka gave a circular nod. "If you say so."

"I'm just kidding," Bridget said. "How's sweetie-pie Leo?"

"Perfect," she said, sinking into a comfortable couch. "But I think I may need to get out a little more often."

"Getting a little crazy?" Bridget asked.

"I wouldn't have put it that way," Ericka said, but knew Bridget had nailed it.

"Well, why not kill two birds with one stone?" Bridget asked, clapping her hands together. "As you know, the royal family is hosting a holiday art event. I know a hot, young Italian guy who could cheer you up," she said.

"Italians flatter too much," Ericka said.

"There are times when we could all use a little flattery. I'm not asking you to marry him. Just enjoy him for the evening. You don't even have to take him to bed," Bridget said.

Ericka stared at her sister in shock. "Bridget, shame on you. I'm not that desperate."

"Of course you aren't," she said. "But you could

use a little fun. I'm looking out for your mental health," she said.

Ericka couldn't help chuckling. "I'm not sure this is a good idea. I was thinking a luncheon or a visit to our museum."

"This is similar to a visit to a museum. You'll just dress up a little more and enjoy the company of an attractive man. Like I said, it's not forever. You could use a little fun. You're looking a little unnecessarily serious and cranky," Bridget said.

Ericka blinked. "That's sounds a bit insulting."

"Just tell me you'll go on the date," Bridget said.

Ericka took a deep breath. She clearly needed to get out. She was getting way too hung up over a bodyguard who didn't want to be with her. "I'll do it."

Bridget clapped her hands together. "Great. I can't wait to talk to Antonio."

Ericka visited with the twin boys and a few of the animals. She promised to bring Leo soon. As she got into her small car, she spotted Treat waiting. She waved at him because it seemed like the right thing to do. Then she drove home. Along the way, she wondered if she should have agreed to the blind date via Bridget, but she hoped it would be a very welcome distraction.

She needed to stop thinking about Treat. Maybe Antonio would help. Arriving at the cottage, she stepped out of the car and waved toward Treat as he pulled in behind her. "I'm going to a formal event tomorrow night. Representing the Devereaux family. The palace will provide a car."

He met her gaze. "This is new."

She shrugged. "Good to know we're keeping the job interesting. Ciao," she said as she walked into the cottage.

Chapter Eight

The next day, Ericka awakened early to the sound of Leo's lusty cry. She waved Nanny back to her bed as she made her way to her son's room. Today, she was determined to brighten her outlook. Perhaps Bridget was right. She'd become too serious for anyone's good. She had plenty going for her. She had a healthy, happy baby. Her child's nanny adored him. She had a supportive family and she lived in a lovely cottage on a beautiful neighborhood.

Ericka looked down at Leo as he whined. "Good morning, beautiful boy," she said, putting her hand on his chest to comfort him then stroking his face. She smiled and he quit crying. After changing his diaper, she put in his hearing aids even though she now knew they helped his hearing very little, if at all.

"I bet you would like a bottle," she said, and carried him to the kitchen where she grabbed a bottle from the refrigerator. He slurped down his nourishment and she helped him burp. If she were following her normal schedule, she would share a little sign language session with him then move on to tummy time, but the sun was shining brightly and she'd heard the weather should be reasonably warm.

She decided to take Leo for a stroll. With a cap over his head covering his hearing aids, even if the paparazzi took a picture, they wouldn't spot anything unusual. She changed into jeans and a light jacket and put a jacket on Leo, grabbed the stroller and headed out the door. The sun was so bright Leo squinted his eyes.

"Sorry about that, sweetie," she said as she pulled the top of the stroller forward to offer him a little shade. She walked to the gate and pushed the button for it to open. Just as she walked through it, she heard footsteps behind her. Glancing behind her, she saw Treat and felt a strange combination of excitement and annoyance.

"What are you doing?" he asked, catching up to her.

"I'm taking Leo for a stroll," she said.

"You're supposed to tell me," he said.

"Nothing personal, but I didn't want to invite

you." She shrugged. "Well, maybe it is personal," she said. "I'm not going far."

"It doesn't matter. I need to have eyes on you if you leave the gate. Anything could happen," he said.

"But it probably won't at seven a.m.," she pointed out. "Most of the citizens of Chantaine don't rise much before nine." She frowned. "This is Leo's first stroll in a week. Don't ruin it."

He blinked and lifted his hand. "Okay. Just pretend I'm not here."

"Not likely," she muttered under her breath but gave it a good effort. She looked at the trees and her neighbor's well-tended garden. She tried to take a deep breath and fill her mind with so many good thoughts that they would crowd out her awareness of Treat. After a few moments of walking, she stopped to check on Leo. The little sneak appeared to be sleeping.

"You little rascal," she said, adjusting his jacket.

She felt Treat look over her shoulder. "Sleeping on the job?"

"I was hoping this would be stimulating for him, offering him a new experience." She chuckled.

"You really can't blame him. He's nicely bundled and shaded. The temperature is perfect with a little breeze. The movement of the stroller probably lulled him to sleep. Perfect nap situation," he said.

She looked up at him and began pushing the stroller again. "Are you a nap person?"

"I can be, but I'll only go fifteen minutes tops."

"When I sleep, I like it to last for hours and hours without interruption," she said.

"Says the single mother of a baby," he said with a nod of understanding. "There's a reason sleep deprivation is used as a form of torture."

"It's really much better than those first couple of months. It helps if I look back at how things were when I first came home from the hospital with him. I have Nanny and she's an enormous help."

"And the solar system on the ceiling," he added with a half grin.

That half grin made her stomach take a dip. She looked away. "Yes, the solar system." She turned silent and fretted over her feelings.

"You don't need to be uncomfortable with me because of what happened the other night," he said.

Upset by his ridiculous comment, she rounded on him. "Of course I'm uncomfortable with you. I tried to seduce you and you didn't want me in return. The situation is beyond awkward and—"

"I didn't say I didn't want you," he said. "I just know I can't have you. It's for the best."

Her heart skipped a beat when he confessed in a double negative sort of way that some part of him perhaps did want her. Her heart seemed to want to ignore the latter part of what he'd just said. Her heart was being very foolish, she told herself and she closed her eyes, shaking her head. "I'm not sure talking about this is going to help," she said, and opened her eyes. "But I'm doing some things to help alleviate my…" She took another breath. "Complete humiliation."

"Ericka…" he said.

She lifted her hand to cut him off. "Please. If we must talk, choose another subject." She turned the stroller around and headed for the cottage at a brisk pace.

Treat stayed right by her side. "How do you like those Broncos?"

She glanced at him in confusion. "Broncos? What on earth—"

"You said change the subject. I said the first thing that came to mind. Denver Broncos," he said. "Football."

"Oh, American football," she said. "I remember that Valentina's husband is a big fan, but he favors another team. Rangers?" she guessed.

"That's baseball. Sounds like he could be a Texas fan," he said.

"Texans. That's what it is," she said. "And Ackies?"

"Aggies. That's college football. They're from Texas, too," he said.

"Where are these Broncos from?" she asked. "Didn't you grow up in Texas?"

"Yes, but I had to expand my loyalties when I played pro for Kansas City," he said.

"I didn't realize you played professionally. Was Kansas City a good team?" she asked.

"They were pretty good when I was with them, but I was on the injured list way too often," he said.

"Does it ever hurt?" she asked. "Wherever you were injured," she said.

He chuckled. "I got injured all over my body at one time or another, so I'd be in bad shape if I hurt all over. But my left knee took the worst of it. I work out every day, but I can tell you when it's going to rain because my knee lets me know."

"How upset were you when you had to quit playing?" she asked.

"I was pretty disappointed, but I didn't have time to mope. With no family left, I didn't have a place to land. I had to switch gears as quickly as possible. Luckily I had a buddy who wanted a partner for a security business. I lived on SpaghettiOs for a while, but I'm eating better now."

"SpaghettiOs?" she echoed.

"Spaghetti and meatballs in a can," he said.

"Oh, that sounds disgusting," she said. "Your palate must be destroyed from that. No wonder you turn down Simon's food."

"I'm sure Simon's food is delicious. I just don't want you to think you've got to feed me. I can handle that."

She nodded. "I'm curious. How do you handle that? What do you eat?"

He rubbed his jaw as if her question made him uncomfortable. "Nothing you would want," he said.

"Okay," she said. "But answer my question."

He sighed. "I didn't want you to know that I eat a lot of peanut butter and canned soup."

She wrinkled her nose. "That's ridiculous. You're so determined to stay away from me in the cottage that you give up gourmet food for peanut butter. Unless you're eating peanut butter and bacon. Otherwise you deserve your bad food," she told him.

He stared at her in surprise.

"I feel better now. And look, we're at the gate so you can go back to your man cave and eat some peanut butter. Ciao," she said as she pushed the stroller to the front door. Pulling Leo up into her arms, she hugged him close. "When you grow up to be a man, try not to drive women crazy," she told him.

Leo looked up at her with wide, innocent eyes and smiled. Her heart swelled with love. "Oh, darn. You're already too gorgeous. The female race is doomed," she said, then kissed his chubby cheek.

Ericka divided the rest of her day between caring for Leo and doing work for the palace. She would likely be out late tonight due to the Christmas Art Show, and she tried to balance the demands of childcare with Nanny so that Nanny wouldn't become overwhelmed. Ericka treasured Nanny's presence and was actually a bit terrified of losing her. She couldn't imagine replacing the sweet woman.

As she showered and fixed her hair and make-up, she felt a mixture of emotions. Part of her regretted her decision. What had she been thinking? She wasn't ready to start dating and she truly didn't have time for it. At the same time, a shot of excitement raced through her when she picked out an emerald-green dress she'd worn pre-pregnancy from her closet, *and it fit.*

It hit her that she had totally lost confidence in herself. Before her marriage, she'd had plenty of male admirers. Since her divorce and pregnancy, when she looked in the mirror she saw a tired woman, dumped by her husband, with zero sex appeal. Because she'd been so busy trying to take care of Leo and make a life for her baby and herself, she hadn't realized how much her husband's betrayal had affected her self-esteem as a woman.

Ericka closed her eyes for a moment then looked in the mirror. Maybe it was time to push the reset button. She was no longer the young naive woman who'd married her husband and agreed to follow wherever he led. True, she was often tired and felt more vulnerable than she liked. But she was stronger now.

Treat wasn't all that comfortable with the event tonight. He was accustomed to Ericka staying in the cottage with the baby. Although he knew he shouldn't care, he did. He worked out, took care of online reports, showered and shaved, but he still didn't feel great about tonight. He needed to keep his feelings hidden, however. He dressed in slacks, dress shirt, tie and sport jacket. That should do the trick. At least for tonight.

He went outside and waited for the car from the palace. He understood that he would be riding in the front with the driver while some Italian businessman rode in the back with Ericka. The thought of it made him lose his taste for everything, but he needed to conceal his feelings.

The expansive limousine arrived and Treat waved them into a spot in front. He held up the universal sign for stop then went into the cottage. Nanny was holding Leo. "Is she ready?" he asked.

"I think so," Nanny said as she walked down the hallway. "I think your vehicle has arrived, miss," she called to a closed door.

The door flung open and Nanny gasped. "You're so beautiful."

Ericka rounded the corner in the hall and smiled. "You're so sweet," Ericka said, and then walked down the hall in a formal emerald-green dress and a cream-colored stole.

Treat succeeded in staring at her without dropping his jaw, but it was tough. She looked more beautiful than a beauty queen. She looked like a princess.

She glanced at him and nodded. "Good evening," she said. "I may need a little extra help getting in and out of the palace vehicle. I haven't been wearing heels much lately."

"I can do that," he said.

"Thank you," she said, walking toward Nanny and Leo. She pressed a kiss against the baby's cheek, leaving a lipstick stain that many men would welcome, including himself.

Treat escorted her to the vehicle and Mr. Italian stepped outside. He was a not-too-young man with model looks and a muscular frame. Treat had wondered if Antonio was just a pretty face, but apparently the man operated several companies.

Antonio bowed slightly then took Ericka's hand and lifted it to his lips.

At that moment, Treat hated Antonio.

"You look very beautiful, Your Highness. Please allow me to assist you into the limousine."

She met his gaze and smiled. "Thank you so very much, Antonio. I appreciate your help."

And Treat hated the man even more.

The couple neglected to close the window between the driver and backseat, so Treat was able to hear nearly every word Antonio and Ericka exchanged. Antonio flirted. Ericka responded lightly. Antonia flirted more. Ericka smiled and sat closer to him.

He couldn't stand it when she smiled at Antonio. It made him want to break every window in the car, but he held it all in. He had a job to do.

Treat escorted the couple into the event for the

Christmas Art Exhibit. As Ericka allowed Antonio to hold her hand, he clenched his fists together. The two of them wandered through the exhibit, studying and discussing the works of art.

After a time, Antonio grabbed two glasses of champagne and offered one to Ericka. She accepted, smiled and clicked her glass against his.

Antonio pressed a kiss against her wrist and it lasted a few seconds too long for Treat. Frowning, he wondered if Ericka was asking for more than she wanted to deliver.

Should he question her?

At the same time, Treat was concerned that Antonio might be expecting more from the end of the night than he might get. He forced himself to block out his jealous feelings and focused on his job as protector.

Another hour passed and he watched as Antonio kissed her hands and drew her against him. Ericka laughed and appeared to flirt with him. Treat could tell that Antonio was becoming more intent and drawn in by Ericka.

Antonio finally took a break and dismissed himself, most likely to the restroom. Treat approached Ericka. "May I have a word with you?" he asked.

"Of course," she said, and allowed him to guide her to the lobby of the art center. "Is there a problem?"

"There could be," he said. "I'm concerned that

Antonio may want more from you than you want to give."

She lifted her chin. "Maybe I can deliver what he wants. At least he finds me attractive and he's not afraid to admit it."

Treat ground his teeth. "I'm not afraid to admit my attraction for you," he told her. "I'm just trying to draw a line of professionalism."

"Enjoy that line," she told him and turned away.

"Ericka," he said, tugging her arm.

The princess glanced down at his hand on her arm. "Yes?"

He pulled her closer and pressed his mouth against hers, sliding his tongue inside, tasting and taking her. She was deliciously sweet in a forbidden way. She tasted like sin and heaven at the same time.

He forced himself to draw back and looked deep in her eyes.

"You are such a pain in the butt," she said breathlessly, and stalked away from him.

Treat stared after her, completely aroused. This *cake* assignment was turning into his worst nightmare.

Ericka tried her very best to pay attention to Antonio, but he mind was stuck on the kiss she'd shared with Treat. Her lips burned, her heart hammered and all her womanly places swelled and moistened. Staring into Antonio's lustful eyes, she couldn't summon the least bit of interest.

"Antonio," she said. "I'm so sorry, but I think I should leave. I'm not feeling well."

"You are ill?" he asked, his brown eyes tilting in concern.

"The nanny for my son has been sick. I hope I haven't caught her cold." That much was true, although Ericka was suffering from a different kind of illness. Complete lust for her bodyguard.

"I'm so sorry, but I think I should go home," she said.

Disappointment crossed Antonio's handsome face. "Of course," he said. "Let's leave right away."

Antonio escorted Ericka to the palace limo with such a gentlemanly attitude that she felt guilty. At the same time, she knew she shouldn't lead him on. They rode quietly through the streets of Chantaine toward her cottage. Finally, they passed through the gates and the doors of the limo opened.

Antonio attempted a passionate kiss, but Ericka couldn't find it in herself to pretend. She pulled back and smiled. "Thank you. I really should go."

"Call me if you change your mind," he said.

"Good night," she said as she stepped out of the car.

Treat took her hand and helped her stand.

As the limo rode away, Treat turned away. "Regrets? You wish you had stayed with him?"

"You made that plenty difficult when you kissed me," she said.

"Maybe I shouldn't have," he said.

"Don't start with that now," she said. "My American brother-in-law once gave me a great quote. *Go big or go home.* What are you going to do?"

"If I followed my professional guidance, I would walk you to the cottage door and go back to my room," he said.

She crossed her arms over her chest. *If he rejected her again...*

"If I follow every other urge and need, I would take you back to my room and make love to you."

She bit the inside of her lip. "What are you going to do?"

"Are you sure you want this?" he asked her. "Because once I take you into that room, I'm not going to want to stop."

Ericka bit her lip. She couldn't remember a time that she'd wanted a man more than at this moment. "Take me with you," she whispered.

Sweeping her into his arms, he took her to his room and bed, releasing her onto his mattress. "You're so beautiful. You have no idea," he said, pulling off his tie, jacket, shirt and slacks.

Ericka's heart slammed so hard against her chest she couldn't find any words to respond to him. She opened her mouth, but no words came out.

"Just tell me what you want," he told her. "Because I want to give it to you."

How could she say that all she wanted was him? She took several deep breaths and swallowed hard. "You," she finally managed. "All I want is you."

She slid her hands over his muscular chest and arms and lower.

"Oh, Ericka, you're too much, but you make me want more," he said.

He kissed her and caressed her body with his hands and mouth. Every breath, every heartbeat made him want more of her. Her lips tasted like cherries and felt like sex.

"You're just too good," he said.

"I want you," she said, sliding hers hands down between his legs.

Treat nearly burst out of control, but he reined himself in. "I'm trying to pace myself," he told her, covering her hands with his.

"Don't do that," she said, meeting his gaze. "Give me all of you."

Her expression nearly sent him over the edge, but he hung on long enough to put on protection. Then he pushed her sweet white thighs apart and plunged inside.

She gasped.

He stopped. "Okay?"

She closed her eyes, then wriggled against him.

He swallowed a groan. "What are you doing?" he muttered.

"You. I'm doing you," she said. She wriggled again as she lifted her mouth to his.

That's when Treat lost control. He just wanted her way too much. Thrusting inside her, he watched her as her eyes darkened in arousal.

She felt so good and tasted so sweet, he thought as he clutched Ericka's derriere, then flew into the most intimate moment he'd ever experienced. He flew high in the sky and wanted more than anything to take Ericka with him.

"Come with me," he urged, sliding his hands over her sweet body.

When he felt that she hadn't gone over the top, he slid his hand between their bodies. She wiggled against him. Again and again.

"Give me you," he said. "Give me you." He continued to rub her sweet spot and she clung to him.

Finally she clenched and rippled against him, her climax producing a ricochet through her to him. "Oh," she whispered. "Wow."

He couldn't help smiling at her response at he pulled her against him. "Yeah. Oh. Wow."

Chapter Nine

"You know this wasn't the wisest thing for us to do," he said. "I don't want anything to damage your reputation. I'm not concerned about my own situation—"

"Oh, stop being a saint and stop trying to play my big brother when you're my lover," she said.

"I'm not trying to play your big brother," he told her. "But it's my job to protect you."

Sighing, she pushed her hair behind her ear. "It's lovely of you to protect me, but I'd rather you make love to me."

"But you need to make a decision. Do you want to keep this between you and me? Or do you want it public?"

Frowning, she sighed again. "I actually don't want anyone in my business. I don't want anyone studying Leo. I don't want anyone analyzing you and me under a microscope. It's strange, but I feel protective of my relationship of you and me. Do we need a contract for this?" she asked.

He gave a rough chuckle and pulled her against him. "No." He slid his fingers through her hair and rubbed his mouth against hers. "No contract. This is just between you and me," he said, then he made love to her again.

At 2:00 a.m., she awakened to silence and listened for the sound of Leo. It took a few moments for her to realize that she was in Treat's bed and man cave. She sat up. "I need to go," she whispered.

Treat slid his hand over her arms. "What's wrong?"

"I need to check on Leo. I can't hear if he's crying. I can't hear if he's okay," she said. "I'm sorry."

"No. It's okay," he said, rising. "Let me walk you to the cottage."

Both of them dressed. It felt odd to Ericka to put on her now crumpled formal gown. She ran her fingers through her hair. "Hopefully Nanny won't be up for my walk of shame, although I'm actually quite proud. How am I going to hide my feelings from Nanny?" Ericka asked him. "She's so intuitive."

"It'll be okay. Just don't discuss it," he told her

as he escorted her from his suite. "She's too discreet to ask."

"That's true," she said. "Otherwise I would blab on and on about my feelings.

"Brush your teeth," he suggested.

"What?" she asked then covered her mouth. "Is my breath bad?"

"No," he said. "Just tell her you need to brush your teeth because there was too much garlic in the appetizers. She'll run. Who wants to smell too much garlic?"

She narrowed her eyes at him. "Are you sure I don't smell like garlic?"

He lowered his mouth and gave her a soulful, thorough kiss then pulled back. "What do you think?"

"Guess not," she said, and flung her arms around his neck. "Oh, I want to stay with you, but I need to check on Leo."

He returned her embrace. "I'm here. Not going anywhere."

Ericka slumped against him for one luxurious moment, and then pulled back. "Good night," she said as she walked into the cottage.

Closing the door quietly behind her, she stood in the foyer and listened. Was Leo awake?

Silence pervaded the cottage. Who would have thought? she thought and walked on tiptoe to her bedroom, listening for any sound, especially any sound from Leo. But there was nothing. She quickly changed into bedclothes and sat on her bed waiting for sounds from Leo on the baby monitor. Nothing.

Unable to still her concern, she broke her second cardinal rule of the evening and peeked into the nursery. She walked next to the crib and saw that Leo was breathing. No need to put a mirror under his nose and mouth. He was sleeping.

Go, go, she told herself and headed for her bedroom. She brushed her teeth then dashed into bed, wishing Treat were with her. His body had warmed and comforted her. Her feelings for him were far more than sexual, and that was dangerous. But withering from fear and need…wasn't that more dangerous?

Stumbling into bed, she fell into a deep, deep sleep.

What felt like fifteen minutes later, Leo's cry broke into her slumber. She checked her alarm clock. It had been five hours not fifteen minutes, actually.

Dashing out of bed, she raced to the nursery and changed his diaper. "Need a bottle?" she asked, giving the sign language for bottle.

Leo's gaze was fixed on her face.

She slowed down and smiled at him.

After a few seconds he smiled and kicked in return.

"Aren't you the best baby in the world," she cooed as she lifted him in her arms. She carried him to the kitchen and brought his bottle out of the refrigerator. He immediately began sucking it down. She was thankful for his appetite. To her, it was a sign of a healthy baby. In that case, he was extremely healthy.

She burped him several times then carried him into the den and put him on her shoulder. He wiggled and rooted then settled down and took a little nap.

"Thank you," she whispered, and leaned her head against the back of the sofa. She drifted off to sleep.

A half hour later, Leo awakened and gave a cry. Ericka shrugged off her slumber and took a sniff. Definitely time for a diaper change. She encountered a very messy diaper and decided to give him a quick bath. Leo had a love-hate relationship with baths, so Ericka always made sure his water temperature was very warm, but not quite hot.

Talking to him the entire time despite the fact that he couldn't hear a word, she bathed him in the kitchen sink. Quickly washing him, she rinsed him then pulled him out of the sink and wrapped him in a towel.

"How's that?" she asked. "Pretty darn good, don't you think?"

Leo nuzzled against her and for several moments, he remained still, safe and warm in the towel. She pressed a thousand kisses on his sweet forehead.

Leo began to squirm. Ericka gently rubbed him with a towel then diapered and dressed him. Putting him in his crib she rested her hand on his chest.

He kicked and played and fussed a little then fell asleep again

When he fell asleep, she was certain she had the best baby in the world.

Treat paced the man cave. He was clearly an animal. How could he have given into his feelings for Ericka? He was supposed to protect her, not ravish her.

Continuing to pace, he thought about the night they'd shared. He couldn't remember feeling such desire for a woman. He'd barely kept his head on straight until that Italian guy had begun to vie for her affection. It was crazy, but after that he couldn't deny his feelings. He had wanted her so much. He still wanted her.

He realized he may as well kiss his plans for business expansion via Prince Stefan good-bye. But he couldn't quit on Ericka and Leo. He didn't know how he could ever quit on them. They'd wrapped their tentacles around his heart. The only way he could turn away from her now was if she officially told him she didn't want him. Treat knew deep inside that the time would come when she didn't want him in her life. How could a life between a princess and a boy born on the wrong side of the tracks in Texas ever work out?

Still glowing from the night she'd shared with Treat, Ericka had to force herself to concentrate on

her work for the palace. Toward the end of her des-
ignated work time, she received a sobering call with
another urgent request for the Sergenian royal family to stay in Chantaine. She had to figure out how
to persuade Stefan to give his permission. Feeling
her frustration build, she decided to step outside for
some fresh air and bumped into Treat.

Her heart jumped in her chest. "Hi," she said, feeling suddenly shy.

"Hi to you," he said, his gaze seeming to envelope
her from head to toe. "Everything okay? I thought
I would check in." He paused a half-beat. "Are you
okay?" he asked and his second query somehow felt
more personal.

"We're fine. I'm mostly fine," she said as she
walked to take a seat by the pool. Treat sat across
from her. "I just received another more urgent request for the Sergenian royal family to come to
Chantaine. Stefan has already said no. I wish I could
find a way to change his mind."

Treat nodded thoughtfully and leaned forward.
"There are a few things you can try. Start out the
conversation with something you've accomplished.
Is there something you've done lately that would im-
press him?"

"I think he'll be impressed with two of the speakers who have given me last-minute acceptances for
the conference. They're both internationally re-

nowned in their fields and one is a winner of a Nobel prize in medicine."

"Sounds good. The next step is to talk to him at the right time of day. When is quitting time for him?" he asked.

"Usually between four and five. Why does that matter?"

"It means he won't have anything else he's trying to get off his plate," Treat said. "Finally, give him reasons that this decision is in his best interest."

"That's going to be difficult," she said glumly.

"It doesn't have to benefit him immediately. The potential benefit could come down the road."

She nodded. "I'll ask Stefan's assistant to look at his schedule for tomorrow and plan to go then. In the meantime, Simon has brought over an immense pan of lasagna. There's no way Nanny and I can eat it. And I won't even force you to dine with me in the cottage," she said, unable to keep herself from making the cheeky comment.

Treat leaned forward and lightly touched her knee. "Ah, but dining with you would make it taste so much better."

In a flash, he'd gone from consultant to seducer and she felt the difference throughout her body. "I've been thinking about you and me all day," she said. "I realized it's not going to be all that easy for us to—" She cleared her throat. "Be together." She frowned, feeling both anxious and extremely uncomfortable.

"I want to have time with you without prying eyes, but Nanny is here five days a week or more. I want you, but I want our privacy. Nanny is off two days from now."

"It's okay," he said, squeezing her leg. "It will be okay. I won't sneak into your bedroom unless you invite me."

The sensual expression on his face made her so weak in the knees that she was grateful she was sitting down. "It's not that I don't want to invite you," she whispered.

"We'll work it out," he said, and rose to his feet.

Ericka stiffened her own knees and walked toward the door to the cottage. "Why does it seem so much easier for you than me?" Ericka asked. "You appear to be in perfect control, when I'm not." Unable to resist the urge, she stood on tiptoe and brushed her lips against his. He swept her away from the cottage door and windows and took her mouth in a sensual, all-encompassing kiss.

He drew back and his eyes looked like black fire. "Does that look like complete control?" he asked.

Ericka tried to catch her breath and mind so she could form words. "I don't know if it's perfect control or not," she said, and then took another breath. "But I like it."

Treat chuckled. "I do, too," he said. "I'll check in on you later."

Ericka returned to the cottage and immediately

fixed a glass of ice water for herself. Like many Europeans, she'd never been big on ice, but after that blazing kiss from Treat, she wondered if an ice bath would be appropriate.

Treat popped in for a few moments later that evening and accepted a large helping of lasagna. Ericka was relieved Nanny wasn't in the room because the electricity between Treat and herself was so strong she was surprised her hair didn't stand on end.

Ericka spent the rest of her evening trying not to think about Treat and preparing for her meeting with her brother. While Nanny took care of Leo, Ericka wrote out every word she wanted to say and when she reread it, she could see that Stefan would fall asleep if she talked this long without taking a breath, so she edited it twice.

By that time, she was putting herself to sleep. Crawling into bed, she couldn't help remembering how wonderful it had felt to have Treat's arms around her. A little damning voice inside her reminded her she had no time for his warm arms and lovemaking, but she pushed it aside. For now.

The following afternoon, Treat drove her to the palace. Ericka was too nervous to chat. When he pulled outside the side entrance, she grabbed for the door. He stopped her with his hand. "Take a deep breath," he said. "Or two. Remember, you're very persuasive."

She took a deep breath and winced. "It's just Stefan is so accustomed to saying no. Sometimes I wonder if it's his favorite word."

"You don't have to take no for an answer," he told her. "You didn't take it last time. Your will is just as strong as his, maybe more if it's something you care about passionately."

She gave a quick nod. "Thanks for the support." She went into the palace. She gave a tight smile of welcome to the staff she encountered then paused long enough to take another deep breath before she knocked on Stefan's office door. His assistant immediately allowed her inside and Stefan stood as she entered.

"You're looking well," he said, and stepped from behind his desk and kissed her on the forehead. "Is Leo letting you have a little more sleep?"

"When he's not teething, he is. I bought a new gadget that hangs from the ceiling and lights up. I think it gives him a temporary distraction," she said.

"You'll have to tell Eve about it. She's got several months before her due date, but it never hurts to be well-prepared when you have an infant," he said as he motioned to one of the two chairs beside his desk.

Ericka sat down and he followed. "You had something you wanted to discuss with me,"

"Yes, first I wanted to tell you about the two speakers who've recently accepted invites to the conference. Hector Suavez, a foremost expert in making sanitary water available in developing countries, has agreed to speak. Along with Dr. Albert Shoen, winner of the Nobel Prize in physiology."

Stefan gave a nod of approval. "Well done. I can see that you were the right person to take on the task of this conference. I'm very pleased."

"I am, too. It also appears that several of the attendees want to put together a roundtable so they can discuss how to make trips to various countries in need of assistance."

"Again, well done," Stefan said.

"Now onto a concern that I have," she began.

"This isn't about your bodyguard, is it? I know his probationary time period has passed," he said.

"No. He's fine. Not too intrusive and he's surprisingly good with Leo," she said.

"Good to hear," he said, leaning back in his seat.

"I've heard from a representative for the Sergenian royals again," she began.

"I've already discussed this. I said no and I meant it," he said.

"What if the royals temporarily gave up their identities and took jobs?" she asked. "We don't have to announce that they're living here, and the whole situation is temporary. They're not asking to become citizens and stay here forever."

"But why here?" he asked. "Why not a large city where they could easily get lost?"

"You're forgetting that their country doesn't have

many large cities. Part of the reason they want to stay in Chantaine is because it's not as well-known as other places."

"That's still no reason for us to get embroiled in this kind of controversy," he said.

Ericka ground her teeth in frustration. "You've always said you want to be a better ruler than our father. Here is a chance for you to show it. He avoided controversy like the plague. You are stronger than that," she said. "This is the right thing to do."

When Stefan stared at her in silence, she lifted her chin. "What if these were your children? Wouldn't you want someone to show some compassion toward them?"

His expression changed minutely. His eyes softened and he rubbed his finger between his eyebrows. "I'll think about it," he said.

"No," she said. "The royals need to come to Chantaine now. You must say yes."

"I must?" he echoed.

"Yes, you must," she said without flinching.

Stefan sighed. "You're going to nag me to death until I agree to this, aren't you?"

"Yes, I am," she said.

"Okay, but there will be strict rules. They can't be seen in public with each other. They'll have to temporarily give up their identities and they will have to work," he said.

"Done," she said, then stood. "Thank you. I knew I could count on you."

He rose to his feet. "I'm still not sure this is going to work," he said.

"I'll make it work," she said, and kissed her brother on his cheek.

"You've turned into quite the soldier, Ericka," he said. "I'm proud of you."

Her eyes filled with a surprising burst of moisture. "High praise from you."

Calmly walking from the palace, she stepped toward the car. Treat helped her inside and shot her a look of inquiry.

"He's going to let them come to Chantaine. I'm so happy I could dance on the roof," she said.

"I wish I could take you to one," he said, grinning at her obvious joy.

It was all she could do not to throw herself into his arms in celebration. "On second thought, I'm not sure dancing on a rooftop is a good idea, but I do know a wonderful little bar on the ocean. I could have a martini and you could have a beer," she suggested, delighted with the prospect.

"Are you sure this is a good idea? You, me in public like that?" he said.

"As long as we don't kiss each other, it should be okay. It's just a drink on a Monday night. They can't be busy," she said.

"If you're sure," he said, looking decidedly unexcited.

"If you can't be a little more cheerful then just let me go into the bar by myself so I can enjoy my martini in peace," she said.

"As if I would ever allow that," he said.

"Allow?" she echoed in irritation. "Just because you're my security detail doesn't mean you have to watch me every minute."

"You say that like it's a trial," he said, tossing her a glance full of heat.

His expression took the punch out of her defiance. She closed her eyes and smiled. "I'm just going to enjoy this moment," she said.

Moments later as they arrived at the bar, Treat watched Ericka pulled her hair into a ponytail and perch her sunglasses on her nose. "Ready," she said.

"It's dark outside. Don't you think you'll look a little odd wearing your sunglasses?" he asked.

"It will make me less recognizable," she said, and stumbled on the walkway.

He quickly righted her. "And if you fall because you can't see?"

"Then you'll catch me," she said with a smile full of charm.

Treat wasn't sure what to expect next from her. From the beginning, he'd known she was a strong-willed woman and she could be heartbreakingly fervent about people she was determined to protect. But that wasn't all. He'd held her in his arms and she'd kissed him with a passion that that made his head spin. She'd apparently just taken Stefan to task, yet now she was determined to savor the moment.

As Ericka had predicted, only a few patrons occupied the bar when they entered.

"Let's take a table by the ocean," she urged, leading the way and stumbling again.

Treat grabbed her around her waist and guided her to a table. "If you keep falling, they're not going to want to serve you any more alcohol," he said.

"Oh, posh," she said dismissively and waggled her fingers toward a server who immediately responded.

"Good evening. How can I help you?"

"Years ago, you made this lovely martini during the holidays. I can't remember the name," she said.

He nodded. "We called it Hollytini," he said, and then listed the ingredients. "We renamed it the Holiday Princess because rumor has it that it was one of Princess Fredericka's favorite drinks."

Ericka cleared her throat. "Is that so? Isn't that something?" she said to Treat.

"Isn't it?" he said. "I'll take a glass of beer."

"Yes, sir. And you'd like the Holiday Princess," he confirmed.

"Yes, please, but can you leave out the alcohol?"

He paused then nodded. "Of course," he said as he walked away.

"I thought you wanted to celebrate with a drink," Treat said.

"I don't drink anymore," she said nonchalantly. "What I really wanted was to look at the ocean while I sit in this romantic bar with my lover."

Her words delivered a one-two punch. In another circumstance he would be all over her, but this time he couldn't. He had to show restraint.

The server delivered the drinks and she lifted hers. "Cheers," she said.

He took a drink of beer. "To Chantaine's Holiday Princess."

They lingered a few moments and Ericka told him about one of the many times she'd sneaked away from the palace to hit the clubs with friends.

"You must have been a terror," he said. "No wonder your brother hired me. You should know that you wouldn't have succeeded in any of that if I'd been your security detail."

"I would have detested you for being a fussbudget," she said.

He shook his head. "Wouldn't have changed a thing."

She smiled and took another sip of drink. "I'm way past high school."

"I'll say," he agreed and paid the bill before they left. As soon as they got into the car, she threw herself in his arms.

"I want to be with you. How can I possibly wait

for Nanny's day off?" she whispered and pressed her
mouth against his.

Treat kissed her in return then pulled back. "We
need to go back to the cottage. Now fasten your seatbelt and stay in your seat," he instructed firmly.

As soon as he pulled into the driveway, she began
kissing him again. After just a few minutes, the windows steamed up and Treat felt like a horny teenager.
Taking a deep breath, he set her away from him.
"We're adults. We can handle this."

She frowned at him. "There you go being all responsible. You make it look so easy."

"I told you it's not easy," he said, his lower body
hard with need. "I'll show you at the right time. Unless you want Nanny to know about us, now is the
not the right time."

She sighed. "You're right. I apologize. You probably think I'm some desperately needy woman."

He put his hand on hers. "I don't. I think you're
an amazing and passionate woman. I need to protect
you, and not just because it's my job."

Chapter Ten

The next morning, Treat received a call from the palace. "Mr. Walker, this is Glendall Winningham from the Palace Public Relations Department. We understand a story with photos about Princess Fredericka has hit an online paparazzi site. The palace prefers to be informed ahead of time of any possibilities of these kinds of stories. We will make a statement if necessary, but I had to tell you because interest in the princess may be elevated due to this story. I'm emailing the link to the story right away. Good day."

Treat blinked as the call was disconnected. He hadn't said a word, but he'd sure gotten an earful from the palace. Dread rumbled in his stomach. A story about Ericka? With photographers?

He pulled up his email and immediately read the story. Who Is Princess Fredericka's New Mystery Man? A dark photo of her wearing her sunglasses sitting at bar with Treat supplemented the story.

He swore under his breath. This was what he'd wanted to avoid. If the paparazzi decided Ericka was interesting, she and Leo would be hard-pressed to find a moment of peace outside the gated cottage. He'd glimpsed the few steps she'd taken to enjoy a few outings. Now that would be nixed unless she was willing to risk more invasions of her privacy.

Rubbing his face, he considered doubling the warning system all the way to the curb. It would result in extra false alarms, but if it kept a telescopic lens from capturing little Leo wearing hearing aids, it would be worth it. Ericka was finding her way of dealing with the delights and challenges of meeting Leo's special needs. She didn't need any extra pressure from the press about it.

After he'd examined ways to extend the boundary around the fence, he walked next door to the cottage and knocked on the door before entering. Ericka, wearing pink pajamas with her hair piled on top of her head and sleepy-looking eyes, looked up from feeding Leo a bottle and smiled.

Treat felt his heart turn over at the sight of her. He'd seen her all glammed up, but something about the way she looked at this moment got to him. "Noisy night?" he asked.

"He had a rough time starting around four a.m. I think I'm going to throw a party when this tooth makes it through his gums," she said. "How about you?"

"I got my four hours, so I'm good. I got a call from the palace this morning," he said.

"I think I may have heard my phone vibrate, but I had to change a diaper and get his bottle, so I decided I'd check after he's feeling more human," she said. "Who was it?"

"Glendall Winningham," he said.

"Oh, my. Mr. Stuffy PR. Bet that was a fun call. Why in the world did he call you?" she asked.

Treat glanced down the hallway. "Before I finish, where is Nanny?"

"Asleep. She'll get up in an hour and leave this afternoon for her night off," she said. "What is this about?"

"Apparently an online paparazzi newspaper has published a photo of you. And me," he said.

Her eyes widened. "Where?"

"At the bar last night. The title of the article is Who Is Princess Fredericka's New Mystery Man?"

Ericka stared at him for a moment then burst out laughing, accidentally pulling the bottle from Leo's mouth. The baby glanced up at her, his little mouth forming a pout, clearly gearing up for a good wail.

"Oh, no, no. You're fine," she said to her baby, rubbing the nipple of the bottle against his lips. He let out a half cry then happily found the nipple and began feeding again.

"Why are you laughing about this?" Treat asked.

"Because it's Stefan's fault," she said, and giggled again, this time with more restraint so she wouldn't upset Leo. "I told him to get a low-profile security man or even a woman, but no, he chose you. No one will possibly believe that you're a nanny for Leo or my assistant. You're just too—" She sighed. "Male."

"So you're not at all worried about this?" he asked. "Because the PR guy warned you could receive additional unwanted attention because of this."

She made a face. "That's true, but I can't tell you how many times they've made up stories about me or my sisters or brothers. Hopefully it will pass soon enough." She paused. "There was only one photograph? If they'd taken one of me kissing you in the car..."

"Only one," he said. "But this means we have to be more careful."

"I think you mean I have to be more careful. I'll try to control myself in public," she said.

"I'm not sure it's a good idea for you and I to—"

"You're bailing on me after a dark photo. The palace will make a statement that there's no mystery man and that you are merely security." She closed her eyes. "I don't want to feel as if I'm begging you."

"You're not begging," he said, feeling torn between doing what he thought was best for her and what he wanted. "I just—"

"I don't want to talk anymore. I've had more than my share of wishy-washy men," she said, rising to her feet.

He blinked at her. "Wishy-washy?"

"Thank you very much for the information. I have other things to do. Good day," she said as she walked away from him.

Treat nearly got frostbite from her abrupt, icy and very royal dismissal. Whoa. He wondered if she'd learned that in princess school. Lord help him if he had to deal with that on a regular basis.

Treat returned to the man cave and focused on his work. He noticed Nanny's car departing the driveway and Simon arriving with food and fresh laundry delivery. The more the thought about Ericka, the more he realized that the woman had a point. Her husband had bailed on her and Treat had given her a ton of mixed messages.

He walked to the cottage and knocked on the door then stepped inside. Ericka was trying to lure Leo into turning over by moving one of his toys next to his side. "Come on," she said. "You can do it."

Sam scampered next to the toy, his head moving every time Ericka moved the toy.

Leo let out a loud guttural yell.

Accurately reading her baby's sound of frustration, she gave the toy to Leo and he clutched it as he continued his push-ups. Sam looked disappointed and wandered to Treat to wind around his ankles and stamp out his human smell.

"Close. Very close," she said, but didn't meet Treat's gaze. "If you're checking on us, as you can see we're fine."

"I came to apologize," he said.

Her head jerked upward and she gaped at him. "Excuse me?"

"I've been thinking about it and I have been sending you mixed signals. One minute, I'm pushing you away because I'm trying to be professional. The next I'm all over you and can't get enough of you."

She stood and crossed her arms over her chest. "Which is the real Treat Walker?"

"You already know the answer to that. Both. I could quit and we could see how things go," he said.

"I don't want you to quit. I want you to stay." She shook her head in frustration. "Can't we just take this one day at a time right now? Can you just let it be okay that you like me?"

His feelings for her ran much deeper than like, but he didn't want to muddy the waters any more than he already had. "Yeah. I'll give it a try."

"Good," she said. "Simon brought Chinese food tonight. Would you like to take it back to the man cave with you? Or would you like to join me?"

"I'd like to join you," he said. And it occurred to

him that she deserved a man who would court her. He suspected there had been plenty of men who had tried to win her over, but somehow he'd had the dumb luck of getting her attention. He wouldn't take the gift of her interest and passion lightly, but he still didn't know how this could turn out without a world of hurt for one or both of them.

Treat and Ericka shared the delicious meal and Ericka charmed him with more stories from her childhood years in the palace. It turned out her sister Bridget had instigated quite a bit of mischief, and the sisters had often plotted how to loosen up their stuffy older brother.

"Bridget was always a fashionista. She was very adept at getting out of palace duties until Valentina and I married our husbands. Then she fell for an American doctor who had become a father to his brother's baby's twins. At first, no one believed it. She's the kind to wear heels on the beach," she said, rolling her eyes.

"It sounds like you managed to enjoy at least part of your childhood," he said.

"I did. We all did. I think Stefan and Valentina took the brunt of the work. It was drilled into Stefan from the time he was born that he was the heir, so he needed to always excel. My mother died when my sister Valentina was in college," she said. "That was hard on all of us."

"You miss her," he said.

"I miss what I wished I'd had with her. I'm determined to make sure Leo has a totally different experience with his mother," she said.

Treat nodded. "Good for you."

"And what about you? What about your parents?" she asked.

He wanted to turn away, but her eyes were warm with compassionate interest. "My dad died young and my mother was overworked. She tried, but I can hardly remember time when she wasn't tired. Between taking care of my brother and trying to make a living, she could hardly catch a break."

"Your brother," she said. "You have a brother. Is he like you?"

He shook his head. "He had some health problems."

"Oh. I'm sorry," she said.

He shrugged. His inability to make life better for his mother and brother was his life's greatest failings. Now that they were gone, he would never have that opportunity again. They were gone forever.

Leo interrupted his sad memories with a plaintive sound.

Ericka immediately turned to him in his baby seat. "Are you feeling a bit ignored?" she asked her baby and rubbed his chin. He kicked and stared up into her face intently.

"How does it feel to have a little person adore you so completely?" he asked

She smiled softly. "It's the most wonderful thing I've experienced. Of course, he doesn't adore me every minute. If he's hungry or uncomfortable or teething, that whole adoration thing goes right out the window. Diaper change, bath and bottle now," she said, and then shot him a sly look. "Wanna help?"

"I think I'll leave that to the expert," he said, and rose. "I'll check the perimeter and confirm that the alarm system is in place." He paused. "I could come back if you like."

She nodded. "I'll see you in about an hour."

Anticipation thrummed through Treat as he conducted his evening duties. As much as he fought it, he wanted to hold Ericka against him and taste her lips again. He'd tried his best to stop thinking about the night they'd shared together, but her memory was blazed on his mind and body. And the more he learned about her, the more he wanted her.

Returning to the cottage, he gave a soft knock then entered and found her sitting on the sofa reading from her computer tablet. She looked up and rose from the sofa. "I just put the kettle on. Would you like a cup of tea?" she asked.

He wrinkled his nose. "The only kind of tea I drink is sweet iced tea. I'll fix myself a glass of water."

"As you know, I spent most of my pregnancy in Texas with my sister Valentina. Her husband is a big fan of your iced tea." She made a face. "I much prefer mine hot with a little milk." She poured her own cup and led the way back to the den. "I was just reading about the surgery Leo will be receiving as early as January or February. I'm terrified that they will have to perform general anesthesia. When I think about it, I'm not sure I can go through with it. But I must if I want to give him the best possible future. It will not magically heal him, but he will be able to hear when he's wearing the external device."

"Will it affect his speech?" he asked.

"It should. Even with the surgery, there are many adjustments that will need to be made and lots of training. We're fortunate because Stefan has connections in Italy where there are several highly trained surgeons who've performed the surgery many times. It's likely that Leo and I will travel there for the actual surgery. Every time I think about it, my hands shake from nervousness," she said, and set her tea on the small table next to the sofa.

Treat felt an odd twisting sensation in his chest. He hated seeing her so distressed. Put down his glass of water, he covered her trembling hands. "You don't need to let this upset you. My mom always said we've got plenty to worry about today. We don't need to borrow trouble from tomorrow."

"She sounds like a wise woman," she said.

"She was," he said.

"I'll bet she was very proud of you," she said.

"Hope so," he said. He hoped he'd been some comfort to her during her hard, hard life.

"Distract me," she whispered, leaning closer to him. "Distract me from worrying about the future."

She was so sweet and genuine he couldn't possible refuse her. He lowered his head and gently took her mouth. Her lips were sweet and plump, her response both giving and wanting. The combination made him hungry, but he was determined to take his time. As much as he wanted to run his hands all over her and sink inside her, he wanted to savor the taste of her, rub his fingers over the bones of her cheeks and stroke her silky hair.

He kissed her for what could have been seconds or hours, but he knew when she wanted more. She squeezed his shoulders and rubbed her breasts against his chest. Arousal thrummed through his body like a drum. Knowing the tempo and his need would only increase, he continued to make love to her mouth.

Her arms stretched around his neck, pushing her into him. He lowered his hand to cup her breasts and she gave a soft moan. The sound tripped his trigger and he was filled with a ferocious need to show her with his body how beautiful she was.

He unbuttoned her blouse and bra then touched her breasts, lingering over her swollen nipples. Her felt her breath hitch in her throat when he lowered his head to taste her.

"Oh, Treat,' she whispered.

Urgency pounded through him. He pulled off his shirt and felt her naked breasts against him. "So good," he told. "You feel so good."

He felt her lower her hand to where he was hard and aching for her. She stroked him through his jeans, and the fabric of her jeans and his became the worst tease. He reached for the top of hers.

Leo's cry broke through the smoke of his arousal. He heard the cry again as Ericka pulled back. They stared into each other's eyes for several seconds. Sam entered the room and mewed in complaint.

Ericka took a deep, deep breath and reached for her bra. "I have to get him," she said as she fumbled with the fastening of her bra. She tried to put her blouse on backward, but Treat helped her with it. His own hands were unsteady from the force of his arousal.

"Sorry," she managed and went to the nursery.

"I'll be here when you get back," he said, and paced the den to bring his body back to earth.

Ericka checked Leo's diaper, but he was as dry as a bone. She knew he couldn't be hungry. Picking him up, she saw him gnaw on his pacifier and she immediately identified the problem. "Your gums are sore. Let me get a cold rag for you."

She went to the kitchen and wet the rag, then lifted

it to Leo's mouth for his to gum it. Treat walked into the kitchen and gave a questioning look.

"Teething," she said. "You don't have to hang around. I'm going to rock him for a while."

"I can catch up on one of my football games if I get my laptop," he said.

"That's nice of you, but he can get pretty noisy," she said.

Treat shrugged. "I can handle it," he said.

"Okay," she said. "I'll be back when he falls asleep."

Unfortunately Leo awakened every time she put him in his crib. Not even the solar system helped. Hearing the faint sound of a ballgame coming from the den, she was surprised that Treat had stayed so long. Any other man would have given up hours ago.

She paced the bedroom until she grew tired then rocked, rapidly. If she didn't move quickly enough, he cried again. She guessed the movement distracted him from his discomfort.

She didn't know how long had passed when Treat appeared in the doorway, his broad shoulders blocking the soft light from the hallway. A twist of irony tightened inside her. The evening had held such promise. Being held by Treat had made her feel so wonderful she couldn't even describe it to herself let alone anyone else. Now, though, she had to focus on Leo. She had no regrets, but couldn't help feeling a little wistful. She couldn't blame Treat for wanting to return to his suite.

"You wanna let me take a turn?" he asked.

Ericka stared at him in disbelief. She couldn't have heard him correctly. "Pardon me?"

"I said, do you want to let me take a turn with him? If you're not afraid I'll do something wrong," he added.

Her heart swelled in her chest and she felt her eyes burn with unshed tears. Blinking furiously, she shook her head then nodded. "Are you sure you want to do this? He's very cranky. You'll either have to pace or rock."

"I can do that," he said, and extended his arms.

Ericka carefully placed her baby into his arms. "Cradle him a little," she instructed, moving his hands into position.

Leo pouted and wiggled. Treat began to walk and the baby calmed.

"Are you sure—"

"I'm sure," he said. "Remember, I can get by on four hours of sleep. Less if necessary. Go take a nap," he told her.

Ericka took in the sight of her big strong body-guard pacing the room with her helpless baby and took a mental picture she resolved to store forever. No matter what happened in the future, she wanted to always remember this moment.

Giving into her weariness, she went to her bedroom, changed into her pajamas and fell into bed. She slept so hard she didn't even dream. Some part of her must have sensed a ray of sunshine sliding past through her curtains, but she had a hard time rousing herself. Finally, she forced her eyes open and automatically listened for Leo, but she didn't hear anything.

Frowning, she rose, looked at the baby monitor and listened again. Uneasiness grabbed at her. Rushing from bed, she raced to the nursery. His crib was empty. Alarm swept through her and she ran to the den.

"Looking for us?" Treat asked as he sat on the sofa feeding a bottle to Leo. "I can't promise I did a great job with the diaper. He can be a squirmy little thing when you try to change him, can't he?"

"I—" She stared a him in surprise. "Did you stay the rest of the night?"

"Yep," he said. "He settled down for an hour twice, so I just dozed in the rocking chair."

Guilt nicked at her. "Why didn't you wake me?" she demanded. "I didn't expect you to stay the whole night."

"Why not?" he asked.

"Well, because," she said. "He's not your responsibility."

Treat glanced down the baby. "He is in a way," he said. "He's part of you."

She hadn't thought he could take her breath away

again, but he did. She sank onto the sofa. "I'm sorry the evening didn't turn out. I loved the idea of you staying the night, but I had really wanted to be conscious for it."

Treat met her gaze. "Next time," he said, his dark eyes holding the promise of pleasure.

Watching him feed Leo, she couldn't help taking another mental photograph. Some part of her sensed Treat wouldn't be around forever. Their relationship was a fleeting moment in time, but with each new day, being with him made her feel a little stronger. He reminded her that she was human and there was nothing wrong with that. He reminded her that she was a desirable woman. She couldn't imagine him wanting to deal with a single mother princess forever, but she would cherish these moments because it restored her faith in possibilities.

Chapter Eleven

Nanny never arrived at the cottage. By late afternoon, Ericka grew worried and called Nanny's house. An hour later, she received a call from Nanny herself. Nanny had been in an automobile accident and had been taken to the clinic for examination.

Horrified, Ericka gasped. "How horrible. Are you okay?"

"I'm so sorry, ma'am," Nanny said. "I'm sure it's just a scrape from the windshield splattering, but they want to make sure I'm not carrying around any extra glass. I'm so sorry."

"Please stop apologizing," Ericka said, worried for Nanny's safety. "I just want you to be okay. Take whatever time you need and get back to me with your progress."

Ericka hung up the phone and struggled with how to modify her arrangements for Leo for the evening. As she fretted over her options, she heard a knock on the door just before it opened.

Treat poked his head inside. "Checking in," he said.

"Thanks. I just received sad news," she told him. "Nanny has been in an automobile accident. She sounded shaken up, but she says she's okay."

"That's rough. Is she being checked out by a doctor?" he asked.

"Yes, of course, but I don't expect her in tonight or tomorrow, and I'm required to attend the palace outdoor Christmas tree festival tonight. Tomorrow the Sergenian royals are scheduled to arrive and I'm to represent my family."

He shrugged. "Do you want me to take care of him?"

"I hate to ask you, but I don't want him anywhere near cameras tonight. With his teething, I can just see him pulling off a hat to reveal his hearing aids. I just don't want to have to answer any questions right now. If my entire family wasn't supposed to be attending, I could ask one of my sisters, but they need to be there, too."

"What about your security?" he asked.

"The palace will send a car with your relief detail,

which you haven't used since you started. Even God rested on the seventh day," she said.

Treat grinned. "God doesn't sleep," he said. "I do."

"You could have fooled me," she said. "Are you sure you don't mind? This is a highly unusual situation."

"I'm okay with it," he insisted. "We'll watch football. He's gonna love it."

So grateful that she could count on him, she reached toward him and hugged him. "You really have no idea how much I appreciate this," she said, her voice breaking.

"Hey, hey," he said, stroking her hair. "What's this? You're not crying are you?"

"No, of course not," she said, blinking back tears.

"You don't have to worry. I'll take care of him. Your boy is safe with me," he assured, hugging her.

She took a deep breath and put a check on her emotions. "I know he is safe with you. Now, I'd better get ready for tonight. Simon has delivered another delicious meal. Coq au Vin. Eat as much as you like," she said, and went to her bedroom to get ready for her appearance.

Within an hour, a guard and driver appeared to take her to event. Darkness was beginning to fall over the island and holiday lights twinkled here and there. The palace would be lit from one end to the other. Stefan's wife, Eve, had insisted on creating more holiday traditions. Bit by bit, Eve was remodeling the palace both externally and in personality. The advisors still insisted on a certain level of decorum, but with toddlers roaming the palace halls, it was hard to require so much formality.

Arriving at the palace, she was escorted to one of the more comfortable meeting rooms. Bridget sat in a chair while her husband fussed over her and chased after their young twin boys. Stefan's daughter sat on the floor calmly coloring in her coloring book while his two-year old tried to keep up with the twins. Eve caught him just before he fell and scooped him up in her arms. Pippa carried her toddler daughter on her hip.

Eve spotted Ericka and moved toward her. "It's good to see you," she said, giving Ericka an affectionate squeeze. "I'm so sorry about Leo's nanny. Do you think she'll be okay?"

"I'll hear more tomorrow, but she was complaining about having to see the doctor, so I suppose that's a good sign."

"I'm glad. Who is watching Leo?"

"My security man," she said.

Eve widened her eyes. "Really?"

"Yes. He's been surprisingly good with Leo. He's not an expert with diapers, but—"

"I don't know many men who are," Eve said. "Hopefully we won't need to keep you too long tonight."

The press representative called them to attention

and reviewed the evening schedule. The children would appear briefly while Stefan ordered the lighting of the Christmas tree. Nannies would then take the children either to bed or to a playroom. Due to her advanced pregnancy, Bridget would be excused early. The rest of her siblings and their spouses would be required to stay until the end.

As she and her family walked toward the large imported pine tree, the crowd cheered with delight. Ericka smiled and waved as did her brothers and sisters and a few of the children.

"Good evening, people of Chantaine," Stefan said to the crowd. "Thank you for joining us for the lighting of the palace Christmas tree. This season celebrates hope, love and peace for the entire world. We are especially grateful for the peace our country continued to experience and I want to thank you, the citizens of Chantaine, for your commitment to your country and to your fellow citizens. You serve as an example to the rest of the world."

The crowd applauded.

"As you can see, the royal family is expanding by leaps and bounds with more expansion on the way," he said, glancing at Bridget.

He crowd chuckled.

"We, the royal family of Chantaine, wish you the happiest Christmas, full of love, hope and peace everlasting."

Stefan gave a nod of his head and the huge tree

was lit. More applause followed, the children waved farewell along with Bridget, and the festivities continued with a performance by a children's choir and a reading from a village priest and instrumental holiday music.

The entire time, Ericka wondered how Leo would have responded. The lights would have fascinated him. He wouldn't have been able to hear the children sing, the music or the applause of the crowd. Her heart twisted. She wanted so much for him. Maybe next year? she wondered and said a silent prayer.

Ericka arrived back at the cottage at ten o'clock, feeling worn out. She entered the cottage to find Treat holding Leo on his lap while he watched his laptop screen. He glanced up at her. "How'd it go?"

"It went very well. I feel as if I should be asking you the same question."

"I let him take the car for a spin, then we went for a swim in the ocean and we had a couple of beers before we got back to watch the game," he said.

Ericka rolled her eyes. "You want to tell me the real story now?"

"Gave him a bottle. Did you know that kid can burp like a trucker?" he asked.

Ericka chuckled. "Yes, and it's better for him to burp. He gets very fussy when he isn't well burped."

"I ate some of the coq au vin. It's a lot better than the peanut butter sandwiches I make, but not as good as your peanut butter and bacon sandwich. We both did some more push-ups. I gave him a bath—"

Ericka looked at him in surprise. "By yourself?"

He shot her an insulted glance. "It's not that hard. You just have to make sure the water's warm enough. I probably didn't do a perfect job, but I figure you can get whatever I missed on the next go-round. Since then I've been explaining different formations and plays. He dozed a couple of times, but I think he waited up to see you."

She sat down next to Treat and extended her hands to her baby. Leo fell toward her and she scooped him up against her chest.

"See? I told you he was waiting up for you," Treat said.

She cuddled Leo and kissed his chubby cheeks. "No signs of teething?"

"Not yet, but it's not the witching hour," Treat said.

"Thank you for taking care of my baby," she said.

"It was cake," he said. "Sam supervised me most of the time except when I bathed him. Then Sam suddenly disappeared."

"I'm sure you could tell that Sam doesn't like the water," she said, then sighed. "I have to get up early in the morning to meet the Tarisse sisters and their brother. Stefan has charged me with emphasizing the rules of our agreement. It's only fair since I twisted his arm. I can take Leo with me and one of the nannies for Eve and Stefan's children will watch him."

"Why would you do that when you can leave him here with me?" he asked.

"Because I feel that I've already imposed."

"I told you I don't mind," he said, rising from the sofa. "What time do you need me here?"

"Seven," she said. "I'll call the palace to give me a ride, but I'm told I'll be meeting them at an inn. I could drive myself."

"Not without security," he said. "I'm going to bed. Hate to admit it, but I'm starting to understand why moms of young ones feel tired."

She stood and pressed her mouth against his cheek. "I thought you're the tough guy who thrives on four hours of sleep."

"That's exactly what I'm going to get. My four hours. Your boy should be ready to hit the sack after one more bottle. If he gets fussy, give me a call. Night, princess," he said. Treat knew she didn't like being called "princess," but the way he said it made it sound sexy.

Seemed like lately the way he said anything was sexy to her.

Leo slept through the night. She almost awakened him the next morning, but restrained herself. Quickly dressing, she grabbed a quick bite to eat and sipped a cup of tea as Treat walked through the door. He looked her up and down then studied her face. "You look like you got a decent night's sleep."

"That's because Leo slept," she told Treat, still surprised.

"And that's because I had a little man-to-man talk with him about letting his mama get some sleep."

She chuckled. "And look how well it worked. I should have asked you to talk with him earlier."

He shrugged. "It's a guy thing."

"If you say so," she said, glimpsing the palace car in the driveway. "I should be back by lunchtime. Don't take him skydiving," she told him, and kissed his cheek.

"Hey, how did you know that was on my list?" he joked.

"Ciao," she said. "And thank you again."

Ericka reviewed Stefan's notes on the way to the inn where she would meet the Tarisse siblings. Stefan had initially requested the Sergenian royals to sign a contract, but Ericka had refused. The siblings shouldn't have to sign their lives away for a temporary stay in Chantaine.

Her security escorted her inside a small inn to a suite on the second floor. When she entered, she noticed one of her brother's top security advisors, Paul Hamburg, along with an assistant and the Tarisse sisters. Both princesses were beautiful, but at the moment both looked tired and irritated.

"Your Highness, Princess Fredericka Devereaux,

please allow me to introduce you to Princesses Sasha and Tabitha," Paul said, performing the formal introductions.

"Please call me Ericka," she said, moving toward the two women. "You must be tired. Would you like some tea?" she asked.

"Yes, please," Sasha said.

Ericka nodded toward the assistant. "Please get some tea and pastries."

Sasha, the elder sister, wore her dark hair in a loose chignon at the base of her neck while Tabitha wore her wavy hair loose over her shoulders. "We're grateful you've welcomed us to your family," Sasha said. "You'll forgive us if we're not at our most congenial."

"Because we've been tricked," Tabitha continued. "We made an agreement with our brother, Alex. He told us he would meet us in Chantaine, but he has disappeared."

"Oh, I'm so sorry. Do you have any idea where he could be?" Ericka asked.

Tabitha crossed her arms over her chest, her eyes nearly spitting sparks. "Who knows? He may be roaming the mountains on the border of our country. Or he may be partying in Italy."

"Tabitha," Sasha said in an admonishing voice. "I apologize."

"I can understand some of your frustrations. I've dealt with my share of sibling skirmishes."

The assistant returned with tea and snacks. Ericka made sure everyone had their own cup and a bite to eat before she began. "It's my pleasure to welcome you to Chantaine, but as you know, we have several conditions during your visit here. These are for both your safety and the safety of our citizens. I'm sure you've been told you'll need to assume different identities. You're not to reveal your true identity to anyone. Sasha, I know you're a talented concert pianist, but while you are here, we ask that you not play in public."

Sasha nodded with a sad expression.

"You can, however, play in private. We'll try to make sure you have access to a piano during your stay."

"Thank you," Sasha said. "It would be difficult for me if I couldn't play at all."

"Tabitha, we're working on finding a position for you within the next few days. In the meantime, the two of you can stay here. However, this is hard for me to say. You must not appear in public together."

Tabitha's face fell. "Never?"

"This is not forever," Ericka reminded her. "This is just during your stay while your country resolves its current turmoil. It's for your safety. Think about it. If the two of you are seen together, it's more likely that someone will figure out your true identities. Think of it as divide and conquer."

Sasha slipped her hand through her sister's. "We

will do what we must, but what do we do about our brother, Alex?"

Ericka looked at Paul Hamburg expectantly.

"We'll make inquiries, but we must tread carefully with the princesses visiting Chantaine. We don't want to arouse suspicion," he said.

"But we have contacts who have contacts," Ericka said.

Paul sighed. "Yes, we do."

"I know you don't take orders from me, but I hope you will give this your best discreet effort."

"I will," he said.

"Thank you," she said then turned back to the sisters. "Now let me tell you about Chantaine."

An hour and a half later, Ericka got into the car and returned to the cottage. She hoped she'd soothed some of their nerves, but she suspected that would take time. It broke her heart to see the fear in their eyes. She wasn't sure how she would arrange it, but she was determined to stay in touch with them. She was also going to make sure they had a Christmas celebration of some kind. After all they were going through, it was unacceptable for them to skip Christmas.

She exited the car and thanked her security man then opened the door to the cottage.

"It's not as bad as it looks," Treat called from the hall bathroom.

Alarmed, she raced down the hall to find Treat and Leo covered in red and blue. "What on earth?"

"I told you it's not that bad. We just need to get cleaned up," he said.

"How do you plan to do that?" she asked, wondering if her baby would be stained with red and blue paint for the rest of his life. "What are you doing?"

"You like art." Treat lifted a sheet of paper with Leo's footprints in red and his handprints in blue.

She reached for the precious image of Leo's sweet baby feet and hands and burst into tears.

"That bad?" Treat asked in a gently joking tone.

"Oh, be quiet. You know better." She swiped at her tears. "How can I help clean up?"

"Just go into the den and let us take care of it. This is a job for the men," he said. Leo giggled and planted a blue finger on Treat's cheek.

At that moment, Ericka felt herself fall hopelessly in love with Treat.

She forced herself to remain on the sofa despite the strong maternal urge to help. Pouring herself a cup of tea, she looked at the "painting" and cried again. She'd taken plenty of photos of Leo, but this was an image she knew she would always treasure. She visualized different frames for the art.

Finally after a few wails that caught at her throat, Treat returned with Leo scrubbed shiny clean, wearing only his diaper. Treat was still multi-colored.

"The bathroom is as clean as a whistle," he said. "I'm headed for a shower."

"Are you coming back?"

He met her gaze for a long moment then nodded. "Yeah."

Ericka dressed Leo and gave him a bottle. He nearly fell asleep, which led her to believe he'd had quite the active morning. She set him down in his crib and he nodded off right away.

She felt a rush of nerves as she waited for Treat to return. The events of the past few days had left her feeling more vulnerable than usual. She piddled in the kitchen and called to tell Simon she didn't want a delivery that afternoon.

She heard a knock on the door then it opened and Treat walked in, his hair damp from his shower, his gaze immediately searching hers. "How was this morning?" he asked.

"Challenging. They're afraid. I can't say I blame them," she said. "I'm hoping the peacefulness of Chantaine will be healing for them."

"It's not a bad place if you need to hide out for a while," he said, then took her hands in his. "You made it happen for them."

"I hope it will all work out," she said.

"What's on your mind?" he asked, dipping his head to study her face. "Looks like it's going a hundred miles an hour."

Her heart hammering in her chest, she wondered

why she was suddenly so shy. "I'm trying to think of a clever way of telling you that Leo is asleep and we have the house to ourselves."

Treat pulled her against him and kissed her. "That's the cleverest thing I've heard all day," he said, and scooped her off her feet and down the hall to her bedroom. "I'll try to take my time, but I swear I feel like it's been a decade."

"It hasn't?" she asked, unfastening his shirt while her fingers still worked.

He kissed her slow and deep, lighting the fire inside her. He ran his lips down her cheek and throat. "You skin is so soft," he murmured and unbuttoned her blouse.

He dipped his tongue in the hollow of her throat, taking her off guard. Another moment of caresses and her bra was gone. She loved the sensation of his naked chest against her breasts.

She rubbed her open mouth against his and he sucked in a quick breath, taking her mouth in another deep, hungrier kiss. His hunger made her hyper-aware of all the achy, needy places in her body.

He slid her skirt and panties down over her hips then followed her down on the bed. "I'm naked and you're not."

"I will be soon enough," he said, then kissed his way down her body.

Ericka fell into a delicious cocoon where only she and Treat existed. He pleasured and seduced her until she couldn't bear being separate from him for one more second. Then he finally slid inside her and they were as close as could be. Afterward, he held her tightly against him, as if he never wanted to let her go.

The rest of the day passed in a sweet haze of togetherness. They both played with Leo and ate leftovers. Treat turned on his laptop and attempted to teach her the finer points of football, but she was too busy soaking up every second. She knew this time together would soon pass. Nanny had already called, insisting she was ready to return to work the following afternoon.

The next day, Ericka found herself sighing in contentment. She couldn't remember feeling this happy in her life. Midmorning, she received a call from Treat. Unusual, she thought. He usually just walked over if he wanted to talk to her.

"Hello to you," she said, still feeling a buzz of happiness.

"There's a man at the gate," Treat said. "His name is Jean Claude and he says he wants to see his son."

Shock coursed through Ericka. She was so stunned she nearly dropped her cup of tea. "Is it really Jean Claude?"

"His identification checks out. But I can send him away."

Ericka closed her eyes and shook her head in disbelief. She'd been so sure her ex would never show any interest in Leo. Why now? Why now?

Remembering what Stefan had said, she felt a surge of raw bitterness and narrowed her eyes. "Let him in."

Chapter Twelve

"I'm here to demand shared custody of my son," Jean Claude announced as soon as he entered the cottage.

Ericka couldn't believe his audacity. At this moment, she couldn't believe she'd ever been in love with this man. "Hello, Jean Claude, I hope you're doing well," she said politely, because someone needed to provide some leadership in civility in this situation. Just beyond Jean Claude, Ericka could see Treat glowering with anger.

"I think you may be confused about the divorce agreement you signed concerning Leo. You waived all rights and responsibilities to your son," she said.

"That showed a lack of forethought," he said. "I

was impulsive because I feared you were trying to trap me in our marriage when I needed to be free."

The way he used the word *trap* made her stomach twist. Ericka had made every effort to save her marriage. "And you are now free."

Jean Claude shifted from one foot to the other. "I want to renegotiate."

"I see no reason to renegotiate. You haven't exhibited one drop of interest in your son since he was conceived let alone since he was born."

Jean Claude stretched his chin. "Must we discuss this in front of the staff?"

Ericka blinked. "Yes, we must. He's my security detail."

"Ericka, I know the Devereaux family has some hidden cash. Look how the royal yachts and the grand palace are always being redecorated. You have yourself a nice place here. You don't appear to be hurting for cash," he said.

"And your point is?" she asked.

"I want shared custody and support for when the baby visits me."

"Support," she echoed, her fury growing. "You don't know what the word means."

"We can make this easy, or I can make it very dirty in the press for you and your family," he said.

Ericka watched Treat move toward her ex and she held up a hand. "You do realize that if you have joint custody, you will also need to contribute to Leo's medical bills. Are you prepared to do that?"

"Why wouldn't I be?" he asked, a hint uncertainty flickering in his. "Is something wrong with him?"

"No, he's perfect. He's also profoundly deaf," she said.

Jean Claude stared at her in shock. "Oh, my—" He shook his head. "Now, I understand why you've kept him hidden from the press. How to explain a defective child. I can't say I blame you. I hope you'll keep him hidden. It wouldn't do anything for your image or mine."

Treat lifted Jean Claude from his feet and tossed him out the door. "Get away from her. You don't deserve either of them."

Jean Claude protested. "Don't you insult me. Don't—"

Treat punched him in the face, sending her ex reeling. Seeing Jean Claude for the opportunistic monster he'd become, she tugged at Treat's arm. "Stop. Please stop," she said, fighting back tears. She turned to Jean Claude. "Just leave."

"My attorney will be in touch," Jean Claude said, rubbing his jaw. "You can't hit just anyone with no repercussions," he said as he walked to the gate.

"I have to let him out of the gate," Treat said, his nostrils still flaring in anger. He did the deed then returned. "Are you okay?" he asked.

"I will be," she said, crossing her arms over her

chest protectively. "I still can't believe he just showed up with no notice."

"The palace keeps a watch over him and it appears he and his new companion have been spending more than he makes," he said as he escorted her back to the cottage.

Treat pulled her into his arms and she savored the protective sensation. "I don't think he'll be back," he murmured, rubbing his mouth over her forehead.

She sighed then pulled back slightly. "You were so angry. I could see it in your eyes."

He looked away. "I lost control. I'm going to have to deal with that," he said.

"What do you mean?" she asked.

"I'll figure it out," he said. "I need to file a report. Don't worry about it. You have enough on your mind," he said, then gave her a quick kiss. "We'll talk later. Put this in your rear view mirror. Your day is gonna get better, okay?"

She nodded, but something about his manner made her feel uncertain.

Treat rehashed the incident with Ericka's ex both verbally and in writing. Nobody was happy that he'd used physical force with Jean Claude, but nobody really blamed him, either. Still, the palace preferred to deal with all matters in a low-profile manner if at all possible. Treat supposed he could have restrained himself if he didn't have such strong feelings of protectiveness for Ericka and Leo.

Pacing the suite, he berated himself for his actions. He had acted out of his emotions instead of with the professionalism Ericka deserved. His partner deserved better. The palace deserved better. Ericka deserved better.

Treat knew what he had to do and it made him feel as if his heart were being ripped from his chest. He sent an official email to the palace, his partner and Stefan. Now for the hard part. He had to tell Ericka.

Treat tried to time his visit with Ericka for when Leo would be napping. He knocked on the cottage door and opened it, realizing this would be the last time he performed this little routine. He found her in the den. She glanced up from her computer tablet and smiled. "Hey, there. I've missed you," she said, rising from the sofa.

She put her arms around him and he inhaled the sweet fragrance of her hair. He wanted to remember that. He wanted to remember everything. Treat held her an extra few seconds then pulled back and took a deep breath.

"I need to talk to you," he said.

"Oh, sounds serious," she said.

"You could say that," he said, then looked away for a moment, searching for the right words. "What I did this morning was wrong. It was unprofessional and I broke my code of ethics by punching your ex.

I reacted emotionally. To tell the truth, I wanted to throw him out the door every time he opened his mouth. I was over the edge when he insulted you. It took everything I had to rein myself in when you held up your hand. When he said those things about Leo—" Treat broke off.

"I understand your feelings," she said. "The whole thing was so bizarre. I was just trying to stay sane."

"Well, you did a better job than I did." He nodded, feeling grim. "I've resigned from my position."

Ericka gasped, staring at him in shock. "What?" She shook her head. "No. No. You can't. Anyone could have responded to Jean Claude that way. He was so degrading."

"I can't be anyone. I've been given the responsibility of protecting you. My emotions were out of control. I lost control. I can't be your security anymore. I thought I could separate my feelings about you from the job I have to do. You don't need to be worrying about what your security guy is going to do. You've got enough going on with the rest of your life. I'm not good for you right now," he said. "I'm going back to the States."

"No," Ericka said. "Please don't do this."

He shook his head. "Ericka, you're not ready to have me in your life and I refuse to add to your troubles right now. I—" He broke off again. "You and Leo mean too much to me."

"But I don't want you to go," she said, her eyes filling with tears. "I want you to stay. Reconsider."

"I can't," he said. "It's done. Your temporary security guy is on his way now. I'm packed."

Ericka stared after Treat in disbelief. She felt as if she'd been spent her entire day in shock. *No, no, no.* She started to run after him, but Leo's cry broke the silence. Feeling as if her world had just been turned upside after everything had felt so right, she automatically went to the nursery.

"Hi, big boy," she said to Leo through her tears. "Need a diaper change?" She chatted with him until her throat closed tight from a wrenching feeling of loss. Then she picked him up and held his sweet warmth again her. Nothing could stop the love she felt for Leo. Nothing. But she'd finally let down her guard and she felt broken to pieces. Even though she'd instinctively known her relationship with Treat might not end with them together, she'd been unprepared for it to end so swiftly.

She'd just grown accustomed to his sense of humor, to feeling his arms around her and just basking in his presence. Her chest felt as if a heavy weight had descended on it. She could hardly breathe. She closed her eyes and his image stomped through her brain.

It was all she could do to keep from sobbing outright, but she had to hold herself together. Leo was counting on her. Within moments, Nanny appeared at the door with a small adhesive bandage on her forehead and a bruise on her cheek.

"Hello, hello," she called cheerily. "Now don't worry over the bruise," she said. "I may be a little scraped up, but not enough to stop me."

Ericka felt a trickle of relief at the sight of the woman although she wondered if Nanny had rushed returning to work. "Are you sure you're okay?"

"I'm fine, truly fine. Thank you, ma'am," Nanny said, then studied Ericka's face. "But you're looking a bit out of sorts. Are you feeling ill?"

Devastated was more accurate. "I'm not feeling all that well," she admitted, biting the inside of her lip to keep from bursting into tears.

"Well, let me take our sweet boy and you go take a little rest. It'll do you good," she said, opening her arms to hold him. "And don't you worry about a thing. I can take the night shift, too. You don't want to get worn down," she said, then made a clucking sound. "Off to bed with you, ma'am."

Following Nanny's encouragement, she went to her room and closed the door. She looked at the bed and all she could think about was the night she'd just shared with Treat. She wanted to run and hide, but he was everywhere. Ericka sank onto the bed and sobbed into her pillow.

Feeling like the emotionally walking dead, she went through the motions of her life. Leo still made her smile, but otherwise she felt joyless during this most joyful of all seasons. She avoided Nanny's worried glances. She shopped online for gifts for her family and visited a local store for toys for Leo and her nieces and nephews.

Just because she felt hollow didn't mean she was going to wallow in it. She bought a few gifts for the Tarisse sisters. Unfortunately, there'd been no sightings of their brother, Alex.

As Leo did his tummy time, Ericka wrapped packages, tossing the cat a shiny ribbon. Sam had been more affectionate lately, as if he knew she was grieving. She scratched the kitty behind the ears then glanced at Leo. He'd turned over and looked a bit disoriented from the experience.

"Look at you," she said, touching his chest and raving over him. "You rolled over. You're so strong," she told him, smiling down into his precious face.

Leo smiled and giggled in return. Ericka felt tears well in her eyes. She wished Treat could have been her for this. He would have been over the moon.

Ericka shook herself for thinking that way. Treat was gone and he wasn't coming back. She needed to face that fact. Her phone rang and she noticed the call was from her sister Pippa.

"Hello, Pippa. How are you?"

"I'm at the hospital," Pippa said breathlessly. "Bridget is in labor. When can you get here?"

"Oh, my goodness," Ericka said, feeling a rush

of excitement for her sister. "Nanny's taking a break watching a television show. How far along is she?"

"Well, you never know with Bridget. She's such a drama queen, but I will say she came in huffing and puffing and she wasn't wearing a drop of make-up," Pippa said.

"That's serious," Ericka said. Bridget refused to be seen in public without her cosmetics perfectly applied. "I'll be there as soon as possible."

Ericka took Leo to stay with Nanny while she watched her television show then rushed to the hospital with her new dour security detail sitting in the passenger seat. He hated when she drove, but he moved too slowly for her. Especially in this case.

Arriving at the hospital, she joined Pippa and Eve in a private waiting room. "I wonder how long it will take," Eve said. "I always get a little nervous when the Devereaux women go into labor."

Ericka nodded. "Valentina gave us a scare, but thank God everything turned out."

Eve continued to chatter, filling the time with conversation about Christmas. The door to the waiting room opened and Bridget's husband appeared, beaming.

"What a healthy mother and healthy baby girl! The boys have taken their turn to meet the baby. Would you like to visit?"

"Of course," Eve said. The three women were led to the birthing room where Bridget was sitting up in bed, her face make-up free, but her hair brushed into place.

She looked up and smiled. "Look what I have."

Pippa took her turn first and cooed over the baby. She kissed Bridget on the cheek. "You look entirely too composed for a woman who just gave birth," she said.

"I agree," Eve said, moving closer to get a better look at the baby. "Oh, she has a lovely pink complexion and that little spray of hair. A beauty," she said. "You did well."

Ericka peeked at the baby and agreed with Eve's assessment. "She truly is a beautiful newborn," Ericka said. "No lopsided head or scrunchy face." She kissed Bridget on the cheek. "I'm so happy for you."

"Thank you, all of you," Bridget said, growing suddenly teary. "I didn't want to let on how frightened I was when the doctor limited my activities. I'm so relieved she's here, safe and sound."

"That's our brave Bridget," her husband said, tenderly stroking Bridget's cheek.

The love between Bridget and her husband was so big it seemed to fill the room. Ericka was happy for her sister, but at that moment, she couldn't help thinking of Treat. She swallowed her bitter twist of loss and lifted her lips in a determined smile.

"We've gotten our peek. Let's give Mom and baby time to rest up," Eve said, and the three of them left the birthing room. "Beautiful," she said. "And

Bridget didn't look a bit ragged. I could complain, but her pregnancy wasn't the easiest. I'll see you and yours on Christmas Eve," she said, giving a quick hug to Pippa and Ericka. "We have so much to celebrate."

"We do," Pippa said as Eve walked away. She turned to Ericka and took her hand. "We need to talk. You look miserable."

Ericka demurred. "I'm fine. Just busy due to the holiday season."

"That's not what I heard. Let's go back to the private waiting room. There was a teapot. We weren't in there long enough to take any," she said, tugging Ericka to the waiting room where she poured tea for both of them.

"I should get back home," Ericka said. "I left a mess of wrapping paper on the floor. Who knows what the cat will do with it?"

"The mess can wait. I'm told your American security man abruptly resigned," she said. "There are rumors that you were romantically involved with him."

Ericka took a sip of tea, but it stuck in her throat. She coughed and set down the cup and the truth just spilled out. "It was a disaster from the start, but he surprised me. He was so kind to me and to Leo. It caught me off guard. I knew I shouldn't get involved, but I just couldn't resist. He was able to resist in the beginning, but the pull between us was so intense."

"He left because something happened with your ex," she said.

"Treat punched Jean Claude," she said. "Jean Claude visited and demanded I share custody and money. He was so insulting. Honestly, he wasn't like that when we first got married. I don't know when he turned into such a horrid person. Treat was horrified that he had behaved unprofessionally and he left," she said. "End of story."

"Is it?" Pippa asked.

"What do you mean?" Ericka asked.

"I must tell you that I see myself in your eyes right now. The misery and loss," she said.

"But you're not miserable," Ericka said. "You're glowing. You're happily married."

"I am now, but only because I went after the man I loved with all my heart. Did you ever tell Treat that you loved him?"

Ericka bit her lip and shook her head. "It happened so fast. I was afraid I would scare him away."

Pippa took Ericka's hands in hers. "How can you truly know what Treat wants if you don't tell him your feelings? You're not a teenager anymore. You're a woman with a child. You've been banged around a bit in the relationship department, but I think you know what you want. Do you think you'll ever meet another man like him?"

Ericka shook her head, feeling her chest tighten with grief again. "No. But I've lost him."

"You could tell him your feelings," Pippa suggested.

"But he's all the way in Texas," she said. "This isn't the kind of thing one sends in an email."

"We have jets leaving for the United States every day from Chantaine," Pippa said.

Overwhelmed by the prospect, Ericka stood and paced the small area. "I couldn't dare. It's almost Christmas. What would I do with Leo?"

"I would gladly take care of him for you," Pippa said.

Ericka's heart hammered in her throat. "I don't know if I can do this. I don't know if I have the courage. What if he turns me away?"

"There's only one way to find out. Let me know when you want to drop off Leo," she said, rising and giving Ericka a tight hug.

Ericka returned home, trying to digest Pippa's challenge to her. She couldn't believe her shy sister had become such a tiger. Ericka took care of Leo after she arrived home, but thoughts of Treat consumed her. She barely slept all night. The next morning, she awakened and decided to accept Pippa's challenge. She was going to Texas to see Treat and she was taking Leo with her.

Packing took little time and before she knew it, she and Leo were flying across the Atlantic. Her baby did surprising well on the flight, taking lots of naps and doing sign language lessons with her on her tablet. Nearby passengers looked at her curiously.

"You're teaching your baby sign language?" the woman from across the aisle asked. "Isn't he a bit young?"

"He is, but he's profoundly deaf, so there's no such thing as starting too soon," she said.

"I'm so sorry," the woman said.

"Oh, don't be. He's the joy of my life," Ericka said, and felt another weight lifted from her chest. One less secret to keep.

Treat sat behind the desk in his cluttered office space and stared at his laptop. Now that he'd messed up the job for the Devereaux family, he was chasing new leads for his business. It was a wonder his partner hadn't ditched him, but Andrew had seemed to sense his misery and chosen not to add to it.

Determined to make up for his failing, he was spending twelve hours a day at the office then falling into bed at night, but rarely sleeping. Visions of Ericka and Leo danced in his head. He didn't know which was worse—thinking about her when he was awake or dreaming about her during his rare moments of sleep.

He slurped down a cup of coffee that resembled tar and added another lead to his list. Unfortunately, with the exception of retail stores, most people didn't have security on the brain. He really should straighten up this office, he thought, looking around at the boxes of files.

A knock sounded at the door and then it flew open. Ericka and Leo swept inside the room. Treat stared at her in shock and shook his head. *Oh, no, he had gone over the edge.* He was seeing things. That was it. Time to check himself into the loony bin.

"Sorry. This isn't how I wanted to start our conversation, but we have a bad diaper situation," she said, and dug a blanket out of the gigantic bag slung across her shoulder. Struggling to hold squirmy Leo in place, she cleaned him, changed his diaper and put him on the blanket.

Leo immediately rolled over.

"He's rolling," he said.

"Yes," she said, smiling and sighing at the same time. "Now that he knows how to do it, he doesn't want to stop."

"Are you really here? Or am I just imagining this?" Treat asked, his heart starting to stretch and fill up at the sight of her.

"I'm really here," she said as she put her arms around him. "Don't I feel real?"

Treat squeezed her tight. "I don't know how or why, but—"

She backed away slightly. "Well, I'm going to tell you," she said, meeting his gaze. "I love you and I want you in my life. No secrets. I know I'll never meet another man like you."

"But I'm not royalty. I came up dirt poor," he said. "I'll never be as polished as most of the guys who've tried to win you."

"Do you have a prejudice against royalty?" she asked.

"No."

"Because you bring it up a lot. Haven't you figured out that part of the reason I fell in love with you was because I could be myself with you? You even seemed to like it when I was myself. You helped me become stronger and more confident. You took my heart by surprise and I'm just now catching up. Say you'll give us a chance."

Treat closed his eyes, feeling his heart nearly burst with joy. He couldn't turn down her offer. He had fallen for her like a brick and he knew there was no recovering from his feelings for her. "I love you," he told her. "Tell me what you want and I'll do my best to give it to you."

"Come home with me for Christmas," she said.

Five days later, the Deveraux family gathered for Christmas Eve. During Ericka's growing up years, she remembered the gathering as stiff and dignified. With all the babies, toddlers and love abounding, it was rollicking good craziness. Bridget's new baby girl was passed around from one adult to the other. Bridget's twin boys couldn't stop kissing the poor baby's pink cheeks. The rest of the children scampered around the room with parents preventing spills and upsets when possible.

Pippa held Leo on her lap and practiced some sign language she'd learned. The sight of her sister adapting to communicate to her son almost brought Ericka to tears. She couldn't remember feeling such love and support.

"Hey, princess, will you skip out to the garden with me?" Treat asked her.

She shot him a chiding look. "Princess?"

"Your Highness?" he said, teasing her.

Ericka asked Pippa to watch Leo for a few moments and walked into the garden with Treat.

He took her hand and loosened his tie at the same time. "Madness and mayhem in there. You Devereauxs sure know how to party," he said.

She chuckled. "Complete with diapers and sippy cups." She looked into his gaze. "Thank you for coming back to Chantaine with me."

"I wouldn't have it any other way," he said, and led her to a bench among the carefully tended blooms and shrubs. "In fact, I have a question for you…" He knelt down on one knee.

Ericka looked at him in surprise. She was even more surprised when he pulled a jeweler's box from his pocket.

"Fredericka Devereaux, I love you and Leo more than life itself. I never dreamed a woman like you could exist. Your strength, your humor, your passion. Will you marry me?"

Ericka was so overwhelmed she could hardly speak. "Oh, Treat. I—I—"

"Don't leave me hanging here too long," he said

"Yes," she managed breathlessly and urged him up from his knees. "I love you so very much. I don't ever want to live without you. Wherever we may go, I want to be with you. Forever," she said

"Will you wear this ring?" he asked and opened the box to reveal a brilliant ruby surrounded by diamonds.

"It's beautiful," she said. "Of course I will." Her hands trembled as he placed the ring on her finger. "The ring is beautiful," she said. "But the man who gave it to me is my true treasure."

Epilogue

Four months later, so many changes had taken place. The conference had been a smashing success. Ericka and Treat had married. Most harrowing of all, Leo had received his surgery.

Today, Ericka sat with Treat, Leo and the specialty audiologist in a small office in Italy. Both nervous and excited, she bounced Leo on her knee. Today the audiologist would activate the external device. This visit wasn't the pot of gold at the end of the rainbow. It was just the beginning. Leo would need to be trained how to best use the device.

"Okay?" Treat asked, covering her hand with his.

She took a deep breath. "A little nervous."

"It's gonna work out," he said, and offered Leo a ring of plastic donuts.

Leo grabbed the first one then tossed it several feet.

"He throws everything these days. It's all that football you let him watch," she whispered.

"Hey, the kid's got a good arm," he said as he gave Leo another donut.

Leo tossed that one on the floor, too.

The audiologist smiled. "I'm going to activate the volume levels on Leo's device now. I'll do it gradually, but as I told you, he may cry when he first hears noise because it can be confusing for the little ones. Here we go."

Ericka held her breath, carefully watching Leo's face. During the first few tests, he showed no response. Suddenly, though he stopped and his eyes widened.

"We may have something here," the audiologist said. "Say hello to your son," she told Ericka.

"Hi, Leo," she said. "Hello, beautiful boy. I love you so much."

Leo looked up at her and put his fingers against her mouth.

She gasped then laughed. "Can you hear me? You can hear, Leo. You can hear, can't you?"

Leo laughed in return and wiggled his head as if he would need to get used to the new sensation.

"That's what we call a late Christmas gift," the woman said.

Ericka looked into Treat's gaze and her eyes filled with tears. He'd been with her through all the up-heaval and challenges of the past few months, and she knew in her heart that he would be there for her and Leo forever.

* * * * *

COMING NEXT MONTH FROM

H HARLEQUIN®

SPECIAL EDITION

Available December 16, 2014

#2377 NEVER TRUST A COWBOY • by Kathleen Eagle
Who's the cowboy on her doorstep? Lila Flynn wonders. The ranch hand who shows up looking for a job is a mystery—and a charmer! Handsome Delano Fox is a man of many talents *and* secrets, and he soon makes himself indispensable on Lila's South Dakota ranch. But can he heal the beauty's wounded heart—without betraying her trust?

#2378 A ROYAL FORTUNE
The Fortunes of Texas: Cowboy Country • by Judy Duarte
Proper British noble Jensen Fortune Chesterfield isn't looking for a lady of the manor...until he gets lassoed by the love of a lifetime! While visiting family in tiny Horseback Hollow, Texas, Jensen falls head-over-Oxfords for quirky cowgirl Amber Jones. They are two complete opposites, but their mutual attraction is undeniable. But can Jensen and Amber ever come together—for better *and* for worse?

#2379 THE HOMECOMING QUEEN GETS HER MAN
The Barlow Brothers • by Shirley Jump
When former beauty queen Meri Prescott returns home to Stone Gap, North Carolina, to care for her grandfather, she's not the same girl she was when she left. Her physical and emotional scars mark her as different—like her ex, former soldier Jack Barlow. He suffers from PTSD after his best friend's death. Can Meri and Jack heal each other's wounds to create a future together?

#2380 CLAIMING HIS BROTHER'S BABY • by Helen Lacey
Horse rancher Tanner McCord returned home to Crystal Point, Australia, to settle his brother's estate...not to fall in love with the woman who'd borne his brother's son. Beautiful Cassie Duncan is focused on her baby, Oliver, but can't resist her boy's loner uncle. As Tanner steps in to care for his newfound family, he might just find his very own happily-ever-after!

#2381 ROMANCING THE RANCHER
The Pirelli Brothers • by Stacy Connelly
Jarrett Deeks knows about healing a horse's broken spirit, but little does the rugged rancher realize that an injured nurse, Theresa Pirelli, will end up mending his broken heart! Theresa is used to curing patients, not being one. But Jarrett's tender bedside manner makes her think twice about returning to her busy life once she is recovered...and staying with him forever.

#2382 FINDING HIS LONE STAR LOVE • by Amy Woods
Manager at a Texas observatory, Lucy keeps her head out of the stars. She's focused on her niece, Shiloh, for whom she is a guardian. Her world is thrown out of orbit when handsome Sam Haynes shows up in town. Sam just found out Shiloh is his long-lost daughter, but he's kept it secret. As he falls for lovely Lucy and sweet Shiloh, can the chef cook up a delicious future for them all?

YOU CAN FIND MORE INFORMATION ON UPCOMING HARLEQUIN® TITLES, FREE EXCERPTS AND MORE AT WWW.HARLEQUIN.COM.

HSECNM1214

REQUEST YOUR FREE BOOKS!
2 FREE NOVELS PLUS 2 FREE GIFTS!

(H) HARLEQUIN®

SPECIAL EDITION
Life, Love & Family

YES! Please send me 2 FREE Harlequin® Special Edition novels and my 2 FREE gifts (gifts are worth about $10). After receiving them, if I don't wish to receive any more books, I can return the shipping statement marked "cancel." If I don't cancel, I will receive 6 brand-new novels every month and be billed just $4.74 per book in the U.S. or $5.24 per book in Canada. That's a savings of at least 14% off the cover price! It's quite a bargain! Shipping and handling is just 50¢ per book in the U.S. and 75¢ per book in Canada.* I understand that accepting the 2 free books and gifts places me under no obligation to buy anything. I can always return a shipment and cancel at any time. Even if I never buy another book, the two free books and gifts are mine to keep forever.

235/335 HDN F45Y

Name _____ (PLEASE PRINT)

Address _____ Apt. #

City _____ State/Prov. _____ Zip/Postal Code

Signature (if under 18, a parent or guardian must sign)

Mail to the **Harlequin® Reader Service:**
IN U.S.A.: P.O. Box 1867, Buffalo, NY 14240-1867
IN CANADA: P.O. Box 609, Fort Erie, Ontario L2A 5X3

Want to try two free books from another line?
Call 1-800-873-8635 or visit www.ReaderService.com.

* Terms and prices subject to change without notice. Prices do not include applicable taxes. Sales tax applicable in N.Y. Canadian residents will be charged applicable taxes. Offer not valid in Quebec. This offer is limited to one order per household. Not valid for current subscribers to Harlequin Special Edition books. All orders subject to credit approval. Credit or debit balances in a customer's account(s) may be offset by any other outstanding balance owed by or to the customer. Please allow 4 to 6 weeks for delivery. Offer available while quantities last.

Your Privacy—The Harlequin® Reader Service is committed to protecting your privacy. Our Privacy Policy is available online at www.ReaderService.com or upon request from the Harlequin Reader Service.

We make a portion of our mailing list available to reputable third parties that offer products we believe may interest you. If you prefer that we not exchange your name with third parties, or if you wish to clarify or modify your communication preferences, please visit us at www.ReaderService.com/consumerschoice or write to us at Harlequin Reader Service Preference Service, P.O. Box 9062, Buffalo, NY 14269. Include your complete name and address.

HSE13R

SPECIAL EXCERPT FROM

 HARLEQUIN

SPECIAL EDITION

*Jensen Fortune Chesterfield is only in
Horseback Hollow, Texas, to see his new niece...not
get lassoed by a cowgirl! Amber Rogers isn't the kind
of woman Jensen ever imagined falling for. But, as
Amber's warm heart and outgoing ways melt his heart,
the handsome aristocrat begins to wonder if he might
find true love on the range after all...*

***

"What...was...that...kiss?" She stopped, her words coming out in raspy little gasps.

"...all about?" he finished for her.

She merely nodded.

"I don't know. It just seemed like an easier thing to do than to
talk about it."

Maybe so, but being with Jensen was still pretty clandestine,
what with meeting in the shadows, under the cloak of darkness.

The British Royal and the Cowgirl. They might be attracted to
each other—and she might be good enough for him to entertain
the idea of a few kisses in private or even a brief, heated affair.
And maybe she ought to consider the same thing for herself, too.

But it would never last. Especially if the press—or the town
gossips—got wind of it.

So she shook it all off—the secretive nature of it all, as well as
the sparks and the chemistry, and opened the passenger door.
"Good night, Jensen."

"What about dinner?" he asked. "I still owe you, remember?"

Yep, she remembered. Trouble was, she was afraid if she got in any deeper with him, there'd be a lot she'd have a hard time forgetting.

"We'll talk about it later," she said.

"Tomorrow?"

"Sure. Why not?"

"I may have to take my brother and sister to the airport, although I'm not sure when. I'll have to find out. Maybe we can set something up after I get home."

"Maybe so." She wasn't going to count on it, though. Especially when she had the feeling he wouldn't want to be seen out in public with her—where the newshounds or local gossips might spot them.

But as she headed for her car, she wondered if, when he set his mind on something, he might be as persistent as those pesky reporters he tried to avoid.

Well, Amber Rogers was no pushover. And if Jensen Fortune Chesterfield thought he'd met someone different from his usual fare, he didn't know the half of it. Because he'd more than met his match.

***

We hope you enjoyed this sneak peek at
A ROYAL FORTUNE by USA TODAY *bestselling*
author Judy Duarte, the first book in the brand-new
Harlequin® Special Edition continuity
THE FORTUNES OF TEXAS:
COWBOY COUNTRY!

On sale in January 2015, wherever
Harlequin Special Edition books and ebooks are sold.

Copyright © 2015 by Judy Duarte

HSEEXP1214

Love the Harlequin book you just read?

Your opinion matters.

Review this book on your favorite book site, review site, blog or your own social media properties and share your opinion with other readers!

Be sure to connect with us at:
Harlequin.com/Newsletters
Facebook.com/HarlequinBooks
Twitter.com/HarlequinBooks

HREVIEWS

JUST CAN'T GET ENOUGH?

Join our social communities
and talk to us online.

You will have access to the latest
news on upcoming titles and special
promotions, but most importantly,
you can talk to other fans about your
favorite Harlequin reads.

Harlequin.com/Community

Facebook.com/HarlequinBooks

Twitter.com/HarlequinBooks

Pinterest.com/HarlequinBooks

HSOCIAL

HARLEQUIN®

A *Romance* FOR EVERY MOOD™

**Stay up-to-date on all your
romance-reading news with the
Harlequin Shopping Guide,
featuring bestselling authors, exciting new
miniseries, books to watch and more!**

The newest issue will be delivered right to you
with our compliments! There are 4 each year.

Signing up is easy.

EMAIL

ShoppingGuide@Harlequin.ca

WRITE TO US

HARLEQUIN BOOKS
Attention: Customer Service Department
P.O. Box 9057, Buffalo, NY 14269-9057

OR PHONE

1-800-873-8635 in the United States
1-888-343-9777 in Canada

Please allow 4-6 weeks for delivery of the first issue by mail.

JUST CAN'T GET ENOUGH
ROMANCE
Looking for more?

Harlequin has everything from contemporary, passionate and heartwarming to suspenseful and inspirational stories.

Whatever your mood, we have a romance just for you!

Connect with us to find your next great read, special offers and more.

Facebook.com/HarlequinBooks

Twitter.com/HarlequinBooks

HarlequinBlog.com

Harlequin.com/Newsletters

H HARLEQUIN®

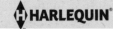 A *Romance* FOR EVERY MOOD™

www.Harlequin.com

SERIESHALOAD